Civil Partnership

Civil Partnership

Timothy Brown

authorHOUSE®

AuthorHouse™
1663 Liberty Drive
Bloomington, IN 47403
www.authorhouse.com
Phone: 1-800-839-8640

First published by AuthorHouse   10/12/2011

ISBN: 978-1-4567-9832-1 (sc)
ISBN: 978-1-4567-9831-4 (ebk)

Printed in the United States of America

For Stewart

Chapter One

'God said the meek would inherit the Earth, not the poor and could you imagine the working classes getting their hands on it?'

Another social observation was being made with prescription and in earnest at the dinner table of Dr Max Hubbard-White in his late Victorian home amongst the safety of his closest friends. The room which was modest for the elegant and well researched abode contained a circular table from the late Georgian period with the chairs, early Victorian. They blended very well. They had been purchased in Chiswick which, as an elegantly suburban area so west of central London it was considered practically Bristol by the inhabitants of Mayfair, gave them added kudos in suburban Cardiff. Max's objective had been to create a forum for stimulating conversation without the need to lean, making his guests comfortable and at ease. It had worked. The table, in Canadian red mahogany shone and shimmered in the candle light making the room glamorous and his friends enhanced. He would smile inwardly as his friends gasped in horror as yet another hot dinner tureen was placed on the highly polished wood.

'Max the dish will stain!' exclaimed Simon, 'put a place mat under it.' Simon was Max's close friend. Half British and half Italian on his father's side he was an architect and loved the idea of preserving everything, even himself. A devotee of the gym and the gin, he had reached an age of forty seven when, as a gay man, he had the vanity to maintain regular workouts but the sense to realise that it offered only limited redress against mother nature.

'It's late Georgian,' continued Simon.

'So it's old' countered Max dismissing his friend's concerns about the table. 'In any event its better it looks used, people will think I'm the type of man who throws gregarious parties where people's comfort is placed before the safety of the furniture. I'm not materialistic'

All the friends laughed heartily at this which hurt Max a little though he didn't give anything away. Dr Max Hubbard-White was an academic lawyer. This meant that he had no rights of audience in any court at all except that of any ordinary citizen but could debate long into the early hours on political and socio-legal issues affecting the kingdom, of both God and the United. He was also a gay man. Forty two, slim yet comfortably cushioned, broad shouldered (he had once stood behind Gavin Henson in the local Spar and was impressed that the rugby star was smaller although more beautifully formed) and loved entertaining his closest friends.

'Max, didn't God mean the poor when he said the meek?' asked Charlotte, a very elegant lady who lived with her husband and fellow guest Andrew in an even larger Victorian house than Max.

'Well He may have but after the affects of universal suffrage and the X Factor programme I doubt it. I think it's only our affectation with material wealth that makes the assumption that poor and meek mean the same thing. We look at a poor person and we think they have a hard life but take away their benefits and they are no less selfish about it than a Duke who might be losing one of his castles to inheritance tax. No, meekness I think transcends economics and frankly there isn't enough of it.'

'Max you are terrible, the poor person needs his benefits to live' offered Sion, Simon's handsome, understated and solid partner of eight years. 'The Duke is obviously rich enough to loose his castle if he has to pay that much inheritance tax.' Sion, as a very able accountant, had a point.

'Yes but Sion who would be the one to bleat about it to all and sundry? I suspect our kinsman on benefit would open every conversation he had with his awful prospect while the Duke may just accept that he had no way of planning financially for the demise of his young and prematurely dead father' Max explained. 'Who is the meek one there?' Max felt a speech within him. 'we don't live in a country that was established in 1832 (he wondered if they would understand the reference to the Great Reform Act and the enfranchisement of the middle classes) and for a Duke to loose his home to inheritance tax is for him the same as I loosing my Victorian semi to mortgage arrears or the Irish.'

'The Irish?' enquired Simon.

'Well give them a chance don't they want revenge? As a nation we are next to them. We're supposed to be a cordon sanitaire against the English but will they see it like that as they river dance up my erring bone garden path with me throwing potatoes at them saying, 'look we're terribly sorry.' I doubt it.'

Max thought himself very good at remaining value neutral considering that his background was working class, but also Welsh. This meant that you were poor, but you read books, saw education as the best way of talking to English people and being convincing and that in spite of any financial disadvantage that could beset you, you always knew that the Jews were fooling themselves and that the Welsh were actually God's chosen people, He having a county home near Abergavenny but kept quiet about it because of the press.

Being Welsh had proven an issue for Max and as he reached middle age he realised more and more that the prejudice instilled in him as a boy towards the English was both unfounded and illogical. His great grandfather had been a hill farmer near Pontypool and only spoke Welsh but his grandfather had married a woman from Bristol and an Anglican. Grandfather being a Congregationalist

Timothy Brown

meant their marriage had been 'mixed' and frowned on
by everyone in 1924.

For Max, Wales was enduring an identity crisis. He
believed the last line of the anthem which states 'We hope
the old language endures' but did not see why that meant
over one hundred million a year should be paid from the
public purse to support a television channel the viewing
figures of which were just under two per cent of the total
viewing figures for Wales and at a time when Welsh was
now compulsory in schools. He was a valleys boy and for
him the effects of post industrialism were still far more
important an issue for the country than the promotion
of the Welsh language. He was, as most were, an English
speaking Welshman which meant he was also British
and part of a United Kingdom. Unity implies diversity
otherwise what would there be to unite he would muse
to himself and anyone else who would listen yet he saw
those with an obsession with the Welsh language as prone
to separatism and xenophobia and this he believed was
undermining that union. He understood the linguistic
persecution which the Welsh language had endured in
the nineteenth century but Wales had experienced an
industrial and social revolution since then and frankly it
was time to move on. English was no longer the language

of England but was the UK's best export. The idea of being able to go almost anywhere in the world, except sadly Paris, and people could understand you was a remarkable achievement. Welsh would never have the same international kudos and was for Max an expensive but yes an important indulgence. He was thinking about this while eating his beautifully prepared dinner when he was distracted.

'Why is the X Factor a reason for the poor to loose their inheritance?' Charlotte asked Max.

'Well its obvious isn't it? such an exclusive programme. The first thing that you must have to audition is absolutely nothing to loose. Well frankly that disenfranchises everyone in this room.'

The group laughed at that and Max sensing that he was gathering momentum continued. 'You also have to have a recently dead relative. It's essential. I thought of crooning a few old Cole Porter numbers at one of its auditions but try as I might I could not get mother to take the pills.'

Howls of controlled laughter at this. Max started laughing himself on the inside but keeping a Mona Lisa front on it all. 'So you see for those who have already achieved something in their lives, the need to preserve precludes them, and we, from diversifying into the mysterious and highly publicised world of the X Factor. People want wealth and fame because they are poor and unknown. It's completely acceptable in the UK as it's an expression of democracy and it's entertaining, but it isn't meek.'

Max was concerned about the obsession with celebrity culture. Mass media in the eighties had provided an expectation from everyone that they could be the new Madonna or Joan Collins and he felt that there was a clear expectation gap between talent and fame that was becoming increasingly bridged by television and the consequence of it producing social passivity. Britain wasn't French and even though the French were finding it increasingly financially unviable to be French he felt they had maintained a sense of religious and political identity which his own country was loosing to the globalised obsession with celebrity. He suffered for it. With his thoughts about Wales's position in the UK in his own mind he continued.

'We are an eclectic group around this table. English, Welsh, South African, Italian yet we all live in the UK.

Why is it that in our United Kingdom we don't have a state of the union address every year? No more than ever do we need one. Our cousins in the US seem to be able to celebrate national diversity in a way we find jingoistic. We have religion in this country but we don't 'do it' like other countries which invariably has made us much closer to God than any other nation on earth, but it engenders notions of conceit when celebrating the fact that it's a British idiosyncrasy. In the last seventy years we have one of the best records on religious and social tolerance in the world and it makes me angry that we don't feel comfortable about extolling that. We gave back India to democracy and that's not how we found it, that's for sure.'

Max was merry with his sweeping summations about the role of the Kingdom in the modern world and loved the fact that he was sat around his table with people who were accomplished and generous as friends. They were proving his point but he always felt that he was being misunderstood. He loved debating nationhood such was the inheritance of being both Welsh and British. Neither word suggested a United Kingdom yet they were both component parts.

The other two guests that evening were Dr and Dr Fellows. The couple was South African but only their accent gave them away. Stefan and Michaela were a consultant paediatric anaesthetist and a GP respectively. They were Max's neighbours, they had two children who looked to Max as an uncle figure and completely adorable. Max loved them. They were his family and knew him well enough to know that his intention was always to make people reflect on their actions with a view to improvement. Max was as a lecturer, a teacher and that job blended the professional with the vocational and Max loved that as well.

'Max do you think that we will inherit the Earth?' Michaela asked. She was Roman Catholic but wasn't too keen on the Pope. Wouldn't that make her one who protests; a Protestant?

'Yes, Michaela but as I requested on my last visit to God's country home (they were all too aware of the Abergavenny reference) I want some quiet village near a lake in Switzerland and that the working class people who, if appeared on the X Factor, might also inherit, be placed somewhere nearer the south of Spain. It's warm there and familiar territory, they can eat, and will be amongst people who love to reflect about how life has treated them and how they have responded to it, and how they felt when they were responding and how they are the only people to have felt about the way they responded, and how they married Jordan . . . oh damn I was trying not to make it about Peter Andre, but you get my drift?'

It was proving to be a successful evening at Dr Max Hubbard-White's elegant and *well researched abode* in the provincial and historic suburb of Cardiff known as Llandaff where, according to the last census, ninety five per cent of the population was white and over ninety per cent of the industry in the area was education thanks to two private schools, one had been frequented by Charlotte Church and choose not to use that as part of its marketing strategy, the other not frequented by her, and did.

As the evening developed the friends drank a charming red South African Pinot Noir which Stefan had purchased especially for Max's recent birthday party and the subject of Max's social commentary was raised, this time by Stefan.

'Max I believe that people aren't taking enough responsibility for their own health and that the welfare state encourages this by making people feel that there is an endless resource of care and kindness that will be publicly funded.'

'So true' Max replied, 'and it's not very meek of people to assume that there will always be a publically funded resource to access. Sion, pass me a cigarette please. Look at me. I smoke. It is heavily taxed which makes the middle classes feel better that years of public education is finally bearing some progress in social engineering, but for me I'm paying for my oxygen tank. In addition I'm covered with BUPA so that I won't have my life disrupted with the potential of sharing a bathroom with someone I would not invite to my own home. I may not be a paradigm in the development of healthcare, but I am taking responsibility for it in my own way.'

Stefan smiled at Max's tangential response but healthcare and nationhood were connected through constant Welsh media protestations that on such a small island as the UK, people with cancer had to travel over one hundred miles, *and to England* to obtain life saving treatment and that somehow this was an appalling indictment on the NHS and each successive Government. Max would rile against such short sightedness pointing out that the only reason he would not travel over one hundred miles for life saving treatment was self deprecation and that would never happen. His sister had recently recovered from a non Hodgkins lymphoma and she had to travel to Birmingham. She had survived and while the chemotherapy had made her sick, at least the afternoon jaunt to the Bournville factory and the consumption of chocolate, (as well as cheese now Kraft had bought it?) had not made her any fatter.

'You could give up smoking!' Andrew interjected. He was an experienced nurse and a former smoker. A double evangelist on the subject and who had that annoying habit of being a bit right. Max liked him. He and Charlotte made a wonderful couple. They had lived in London and had been privately educated. They had played the property market thanks to Charlotte's estate agent mother Marianne and had done well from it. Evenings at their home evolved without pretention as the best food and the most appropriate wines were served. Max would marvel at their ability to prepare food, even courses as you sat in their enormous kitchen and talked about life. He was not so relaxed in his preparations which always involved an early start and whisky. For him the preparation of dinner was something that had to be concluded by seven o' clock so he could relax and wait for his guests.

'True' Max's eyebrows rose at the thought of such a harsh and prescriptive idea. He often reflected on the vast number of clinically obese people who shared Andrew's thoughts on smoking and who never saw the irony. 'However, this poses an equitable dilemma Andrew.' Max continued. 'If I smoke, I run the risk of killing myself perhaps prematurely, although as a man at forty two I have already surpassed the biblical three score and ten in gay years. If I do not smoke, the X Factor, the lack of meekness in society and incorrectly conjugated verbs in the media may all conspire against me and I'll end up killing someone else. That, I feel, would be legally wrong. Have you got a light Sion?'

Andrew shook his head and grinned at Max. Max often sparred with him but they were friends and Max admired the way he dealt with everyone in his family. He was renaissance man and was so logical about everything. He took control, read well, was good with his hands and seemed to be the doting husband and father. Max was proud of their friendship.

The table knew Max had won and lost points in his argument but they were friends, they accepted, they knew him and they cared. Max loved them in his home and they loved being entertained there. The olive green room, tastefully decorated thanks to Masers Farrow and Ball provided a perfect setting for dinner and the frosted lighting that hung like a suspended discreet bauble not eight inches over the centre of the Georgian table reflected not just the shimmer of the candles nearby but also the gloss of the women and the shine of the men.

The friends had all met through Max, who as a Valley's boy had been confirmed by his family as having achieved as he now lived in a five bedroom home in Cardiff, a city twenty five miles away from his birth place, and light years away from his childhood. The host for the evening had met a beautiful young man eighteen months ago after his first partner died four years prior of an embolism brought on by Parkinson's disease. His new partner's name was Cameron, a slim man with a big smile, penetrating eyes, strawberry blond hair and an enormous energy for living. Max loved him and loved him as a grown up should love and his friends loved him. Cameron always laughed infectiously at Max's observations and tonight was no exception. Max was on form.

'Stefan' Max said, 'you are an accomplished man who earns a six figure salary. You often tell me stories about your work. The baby with a malignant tumour the size of its leg, the parents who get upset with you because you can't tell them there and then that the child will be fine and that there will be no further complications, the suffering, the ingratitude, the classic expectation gap between the learned professional and the emotional amateur. Whenever I need a light fitting fixed, I get my friendly straight neighbour to come and do it. The trade off is that whenever you need your lights cleaning (the couple had suffered from a lack of staff after they left South Africa), I am there. I think that is meekness. I think you are meek. Of course according to Sion you may be a lot meeker if your pay is cut.' Sion was an accountant with the NHS and had often commented on the size of salaries given to such accomplished men and women.

'Max you are using my words out of context' Sion protested but with a grin and a blush on his face that showed forgiveness, for now anyway. Stefan smiled too knowing Max was teasing him and aware of the political realism behind the smiles. Funding accomplished men and women and meeting waiting list objectives had allowed many anaesthetists the opportunity of doubling their salaries before the formula for paying them had changed in the NHS.

Charlotte had met Stefan and Michaela when she sold them the house next to Max's. He had owned his neighbours house before buying his current home five years ago from his then neighbours. They had been twins. At ninety four, one of the oldest living twins in Wales but not the oldest. It was the best thing he had done and here they were this evening enjoying the warmth of friendship and digesting the wonderful food and the albeit vandalising china.

The four, Andrew, Charlotte, who also had two beautiful children, and Drs Fellows were now camping companions (viewed with knitted brows by Max who had suggested that 'glamping' might coax him to accept an invitation to join) and would often be guests at each others homes where Max and Cameron were always welcomed.

This was middle Wales. Diverse, international and regardless of sexual orientation. Max wondered whether he could get Assembly Government funding for the dinner on the basis of diversity but as the AMs only worked four days a week (well Wales is small) it had been difficult to synchronise diaries. Max refrained, believing that the money could be given to Merthyr Tydfil, a valley's town in greater need than his dinner guests. Max had also experienced government funding on diversity issues. At the last Mardi Gras event, money was given for an exploration of gay culture by purchasing fifteen pairs of Shirley Bassey's shoes. Max had rolled his eyes at the time.

'Max, why this obsession with meekness suddenly? asked Andrew,' I don't always perceive you as a meek person. You drive a BMW 645i convertible, you live in a large home and you dress in a way that suggests that you are moneyed.'

'Andrew!' Max was about to pounce on this. 'The other day I ventured into town. As you know I go on a Wednesday when the demographics are at their safest. Unfortunately quite a few people had slipped through the net and also ventured in probably in breach of their electronic tagging, which caused me to think again about health and safety issues. Anyhuw I remembered my paternal grand mother. She was a stout lady in her sixties who believed that a mix grill should come with a side order of pasty and chips. We ate on Friday and were contained at home until Sunday lunch. Week ends were often predictable. When she shopped, always on a Thursday so that the fresh foods would not spoil by the week end, she wore a hat and gloves. She was not a beautiful woman but she looked so elegant and so, well, beautiful, that we loved and loved her. She was humble and meek. The reason? She never assumed that just turning up expressing your own sense of comfort and, if I may gulp, style, was enough. She always made an effort to look as good as she could'

'So? Andrew was curious.

Max continued 'I always believed then that being smart meant that you turned up well mannered and that whether you were attending a royal ball or just shopping, there was always a code of dress which might make others have respect for you and that's because you were showing them courtesy. I believe that is actually meekness and wonderfully expressed. Today in town I witnessed four men, on separate occasions who chose instead to express their underwear which made up for the fact that their jeans were at half mast as though Levis, Wrangler and Armani were in mourning. I then noticed a young woman who had taken the concept of leggings and had applied it all the way up to her neck. She was a smoker, so of course I afforded her the tribal margins but all it emphasised was that she went out at the neck and refused to come in again until she reached her ankles. I'm gay, Andrew, and strategic about shopping trips but such sights weren't worth the ten per cent discount at John Lewis, I'm sorry'

The friends giggled at this, the wine causing Simon to snort as he reflected on his own angst with the complete lack of circumspection in society. Max continued 'You see the X Factor encourages everyone to think they are special. Not in the eyes of God as for they He is not constantly telling them they will be stars and are the best thing He has ever heard, but for a much more sinister objective which is to believe that if you are not a celebrity then somehow you won't be special. It lacks trust in faith and I believe it is something which is symbiotic. It extols glamour, fame and even talent at some point but it also sends the message that this is the ultimate objective. After all it is called the X Factor. Is there a mathematician that could tell us what X actually stands for here? Is it God like?'

The friends were people that were anti X factor, not that it wasn't present in a few of their homes on a Saturday night. It was entertaining but when Sion referred to a 'Marco' or a 'Cheryl' Max had to ask if it was one of Simon's Italian relatives or the domestic help before the look of concern on Sion's face for Max's lack of knowledge in *current affairs* told him that yet again he was referring to one of the optimistically entitled contestants on the programme. No, it was that here sat the backbone of the country; the middle classes, worried about their jobs, their children, their homes, their taxes, their security. Here there would be no hand-up from a television programme. Here was real life, to be enjoyed yet that enjoyment was to be paid for with responsibility, consistency and endurance; everyone sane, everyone strong. Validation at this dining table came from within first. Yet this evening, and Max loved this the most, everyone would know just how much they were worth if not to the country then to him. He was a happy man indeed.

Max then made an announcement. In the demeanour of the most humble of curates he said, 'We are gathered here this evening to bear witness to the fact that I have asked my beautiful partner, Cameron to enter into a civil partnership with me and he has graciously accepted. We are registered at Fortnums and the local Spar. We are nothing if not inclusive.'

Max had not expected the next reaction but his friends, these wonderful achieving individuals all stood and applauded. Max beamed and for a moment had to stop himself from showing emotion. Cameron stood and kissed him on the cheek. Public displays of affection were something about which Max felt uncomfortable but on this occasion he let go to the moment as one by one his friends all kissed him on the cheek. Man, woman, straight, gay, all with the same reaction, all with the same sense of joy that they were to be the first to be told. Max waved his arms up and down gesturing for them to re take their seats.

'It will be a quiet affair. I am over forty and therefore discretion is everything but we decided that we not only love each other but we want to make a commitment to each other in front of our family and our closest friends. We are not having a pre-nup and Cameron is happy about that as it means that he will now jointly own the art.'

Cameron prodded Max and laughed loudly as did the others. Max continued, 'Five years ago I lost my partner.

I had the privilege at that time of being with him the moment he died. I never thought I would be able to feel that sort of privilege again but this evening I do. I am not marrying Cameron because I love him, I could do that very easily without any sort of legal validation but I want him to be my next of kin, my legal partner and give him all the security that brings. I do not believe that marriage or civil partnership is primarily a romantic union, but I hope you all understand that I love him very much and this I believe remains the best expression of that love. I hope you will all attend. It will be in August, City Hall for the ceremony and our home for the reception.'

Stefan said, 'Max on behalf of all of us, congratulations. You look very happy and Michaela and I have seen such a change in you these past eighteen months. We will be there of course. I shall change my work schedule for it.'

Max was all too aware of how much things had altered since he met Cameron and for a moment had to check himself once more from emotions. The first three years after Robert's death had been the worst but this evening was not about looking back but about going forward. He and Cameron were there now ready to move forward together. This would be their civil partnership.

Chapter Two

The following day Simon invited Max to have coffee in the area known as Pontcanna. It was technically Riverside but to mention this would cause an immediate state of emergency amongst the local estate agents not to mention apoplectic fits amongst the over privileged inhabitants. The local tourist board had described it as a multi cultural area of the city. Max, having often experienced the Latin Quarter in Paris, felt it was more like a street with some nice shops and cafes. However he was still on a high after the previous evening and wasn't going to judge others' perceptions. Remain circumspect. God did not give you the *locus standi* to make quasi omnipotent judgements about others' points of view, no matter how wrong they were! He always enjoyed Simon's company. Simon always made an effort in any social gathering which Max decided made him one of the last noblemen.

They shared many similarities, both over forty with stable jobs. Simon worked for the local museum as an architect and designer and had done, Max pondered, since the place was built. They were both gay and now enjoyed sharing their lives with younger (and more attractive) men. They were both concerned about the lack of manners in society and they always found something at which to laugh whenever they met. Max identified with Simon more than anyone else.

'So' started Simon, 'you are going to be married. That was quite an announcement. Does he know you're broke?'

Max was ruffled by this but responded with dignity. 'It's a civil partnership and I own a million pounds worth of property in this city and unlike London where it means you have an en-suite and your neighbours all speak English, here it still means something. Yes he does know the situation. Thank you very much for asking.'

'Oh I don't mean anything by it,' Simon sounded defensive, 'its just that there have been others who have taken advantage since Robert's death and I just didn't want you to get hurt.'

Max knew Simon was blunt but sincere in his concern. When Robert had died he and Sion had been the first people there and Simon had even let Max smoke in their kitchen that night, a truly remarkable gesture for a man who refused to buy duty free for anyone.

'Simon, he knows everything and doesn't judge me. He makes me strong and he makes me good. Just be happy.'

'I am,' said Simon very quickly, Sion and I were wondering what to wear is all.'

'Oh come in jeans and a T shirt. Wear a pair of chaps if you like but make sure you wear pants with them. It is City Hall and the seats are leather.' The pair giggled a bit as their cappuccinos arrived. It was 10.30 am and as half Italian, Simon would not touch such a milky drink after eleven. It would be a breach of etiquette for him.

They sipped the foam and as they did Max thought about Simon's words. He had a point, to a point. There had been some bad experiences since Robert died. The Pole, who belied his country's reputation of hard work by being the most stationery of individuals. Max remembered the trip the two had taken to Warsaw and the recognition that entitlement can come from a deprived background especially when you are then faced with the comparative wealth of the UK. The young man had been attractive but his characteristic passive attitude continued on the more intimate front. Max would gently run his hand down the Pole's arm. It wasn't fore play he was checking for a pulse. Max smiled and said to Simon' 'Do you know how many paramedics I have on my Christmas card list?' Simon looked perplexed.

'Sion and I are really pleased for you' Simon continued.
'Really?' asked Max, 'Yet you and Sion after eight years have no such plans?'
'I said I'm happy for you, not that I believe in marriage,' Simon replied.

Simon and Sion were two men that like so many of Max's friends were a very private couple. It was always a privilege when they shared something about themselves with anyone as Max knew it was a sign of trust. He appreciated the moments when they would turn to him to relay a story about an argument or about a sexual faux pas. Not often would they do this but enough to let Max know that they considered him a close friend.

The four, Simon and Sion, Max and Cameron, would always end up laughing over some incident. They were two happy couples who had differing views on commitment and how it should be expressed and Max knew not to challenge their differences. As an academic lawyer Max had once offered Simon and Sion advice concerning how they should buy their current home. He had told them, 'Ensure the equitable estate is tenants in common and not joint tenants and make a will.' Sion as the younger man of thirty one had contributed less to the purchase price walked out of Max's home at that point. Max had been mortified and knew from then on to respect others' boundaries. He would never forget that.

Yet he couldn't help thinking. So many people co-habit these days as their relationships seem to just evolve. People seem to think that their legal rights evolve with them which Max thought was arrogant, but in the absence of marriage a non legal owning co-habitee has a great up hill task in establishing an interest in their partner's home even when they had made a significant contribution to it for many years.

He would often stand in front of his class extolling the virtues of marriage. 'Ladies', he would begin. 'I am now going to sound like a televangelist lawyer. There are two claims you can make over a man's home if you are not married. One is to hope he dies and has put you in the will. The other is that you split up and you try to claim a resulting or constructive trust.' These are not claims Max would recommend so he would ask his students, 'Doesn't marriage give clarity on the situation? You have the security to love better if you know you don't have to undertake a detailed policy on what will happen if the relationship ends. I know the feminists think it's servile to be wedded to a husband but most of them have transferrable skills not to mention high incomes. What about the blue collar woman when she splits from her man, if marriage doesn't give her rights it's a case of dog eat dog' Yet how many women and increasingly men would sleep with someone for a long time and still feel inhibited to talk about any property rights they may have acquired in their partner's home.

Max would then relay to his class the case of James v Thomas, a recent decision which illustrated Max's concerns. The claimant, a woman who had been with her partner for eighteen years and made 'Herculean' efforts in her partner's business and loaned him five thousand pounds failed to get anything from the courts when they split as her intentions regarding the property did not meet the strict legal criteria of the aforementioned trusts. The case had only been brought not because the defendant did not want her to get anything but disputed the percentage of the property for which she was asking. She ended up with nothing from the courts.

Max would continue with his class, 'It all seems a bit grabby asking about rights when you're in *lurrve* but when day breaks and the relationship ends, what then? Marriage, marriage, marriage. It's a legal choice so take advantage. I don't want any of my young women to come back in ten years time and say, 'Dr White, it's over, and I've lost everything and we were so in love.' Max loved giving his students parental advice and they would love to listen.

Simon had almost finished his cappuccino. He was a fast drinker in spite of his ability to talk at length about things and make very opinionated evaluations. 'So will you enter into a pre-nup?' he asked.

'No, definitely not' replied Max. 'I am not a wealthy man and Cameron has nothing but if I am going to commit then it has to be completely. We are getting married not doing the hokey kokey.'

'You put your whole self into that at the end' Simon continued.
'True,' replied Max, 'but my marriage will have my whole self from the beginning.'
'Where will you go on honeymoon?' Simon asked.

'Oh I don't know. A European city, you know I am not a beach person.' Max thought about them for a moment. When travelling to Paris he would see them at Cardiff International Airport in their flip flops prospective in their use when it was minus one outside. The travellers beaming a certain conceited smile as the announcement for the flight to Alicante would ring through the departure lounge. The passengers, often fat with no inhibitions, would clip clip it up to the gate and Max would wonder how Britain had ever attained an Empire.

'I know Simon, I've never been to Copenhagen. What do you think?'

'Wonderful, wonderful!' Simon replied with a cheeky grin. The two ordered more cappuccinos as it was only 10.50 and sat looking at the street in Pontcanna. Anywhere else in Wales it would have a nice Victorian terrace, unassuming yet elegant. The Camden of Cardiff perhaps or maybe Islington. Somewhere abouts. Yet here, the houses were the hub of A list media types. The BBC was only a mile and a half away and this is where the top earners lived. A five bedroom terrace was half a million with often no parking, the four beds around four hundred thousand. Nothing by London standards but this was Cardiff and here was the epicentre of the media's professional elite. Max felt a little churned up inside. He wasn't sure if it was the cappuccinos (two was excessive) or the fact that twenty years ago you could have bought four of the five beds for half a million. If only he had had the nerve. Still now he was getting civil partnered so he sighed and enjoyed just being for a moment.

Just then Max heard his name called, 'Max! Dear, how are you?' It was Marianne, Charlotte's mother. She was tottering along the street armed with two shopping bags and a knowing look in her eye. Max was pleased, yet apprehensive to see her.

'Marianne, how lovely to see you. I see you're getting the economy back on track. I'll be able to get credit again soon at this rate.' Marianne laughed nervously at that comment. She was an interesting woman. At nearly seventy she had maintained her figure and was glamorous. Blonde hair neatly quaffed with an air that suggested that life was fine and wonderful. This belied the fact that three years prior she had been in a very acrimonious break up with her partner who had left her for a much younger woman from somewhere in Africa. Marianne had been devastated, and the incident had left a terrible scar. She had wonderful support from her family. Charlotte and Andrew had even taken her in to help out financially, as she was in business with her partner and the break up had been damaging. Marianne was in pain and Max knew this, so he afforded her wide margins when, on times, she could be completely insensitive about the feelings of others. She had been a business woman in the days when banks would be suspicious of lending a woman money when she already had a husband and children, but Marianne had spent a lifetime buying and selling property successfully and had sold Max his first home in Llandaff. He liked her and he respected her. Max breathed deeply and hoped for the best.

'Marianne you look wonderful,' Max said.

'Thank you dear I've just had my hair done. Charlotte called me this morning and told me the news. I am so happy for you. You know Basil was asking after you at the salon.'

Max winced. Basil had been a neighbour of Max's when he first moved to Cardiff. The area was Grangetown, often referred to by estate agents as 'Up and Coming' due to its close proximity to the city centre. Max had bought his first home in City Gardens. A walled enclave referred to as 'posh' by the outsiders. It was a neat estate and Max had bought in a cul-de-sac of thirty four two and three bedroom homes. Of the thirty four homes on his street, fifteen were occupied by gay men and women leading the taxi drivers to refer to it as either Fairy Towers or the more pejoratively Sissy Gardens. Max didn't mind, his own friends visiting from London would comment on the high level of Asians in the area referring to the suburb as Grangestahn. It was all very amusing and harmless.

Basil was gay and was the son of a wealthy businessman and was very beautiful, thanks to both inherited bone structure and Dr Willis, a local plastic surgeon specialising in rhinoplasty. Max had learned early on that the criteria often resulted in a complete inability to make an effort with people, although Basil had invited him a few times for a drink more out of curiosity than anything nefarious. That was sixteen years ago and Max was surprised that Basil would even remember him.

'Well Marianne, that's lovely,' Max nearly lied, but he had an inkling of pleasure in the fact. Basil had been a catch for the typically aesthetic yet shallow gay man and Max felt a shudder of ego.

'You know he doesn't have a partner and he is such a lovely boy.'
'Boy, Marianne he's my age.'
'Dear you're all boys to me. He's such a handsome man you know.'
'Marianne, Charlotte did tell you I'm getting 'married' and not that I've won the lottery didn't she?'
'Yes dear.' Marianne looked perplexed.
'Well I'm sure Basil will find someone. I did and I'm really happy.'
'Are you sure Max,' Marianne continued.
'I am' Max confirmed, teeth slightly grating.
'Well dear I am as well,' Marianne said.
'Good,' Max countered assertively, wounded that after feeling so happy about his own news that someone felt

the need to fix him up with their hairdresser or indeed anyone else.

'Well Marianne I hope you can come to the wedding,' Max offered more to get the subject back onto his happiness.

'Yes dear, I'll be there.'

'And be sure to tell Basil how happy I am. Send my best,' Max said quite insincerely.

'I shall,' Marianne promised equally insincerely.

After she had gone it was Simon that made the first statement. 'Well that was rude.'

'Oh it's the depression. It can paralyse the thought process, I hope.'

'I know but really she was trying to fix you up,' Simon countered.

'Perhaps she's on commission, she's been selling old properties for a long time,' Max offered. Simon giggled at that but looked straight at Max.

'Well is she really coming to the wedding?' Simon asked.

'Of course she is. I've known her and her family for over twelve years. Weddings are about history. Your friends, family, your past and Marianne is an important part of that. It would be totally unkind of me to exclude her. She may have impliedly disrespected the fact that I've chosen my partner but you know she genuinely has gone away thinking she has given me an option for being happy. I really believe that.' Max sounded convincing but wasn't.

'Well I think you're very generous,' Simon said with affection and disbelief.
'No, it's the right thing to do,' Max said more confidently. 'I like her.'

The two friends finished their drinks and ambled through the park back to Max's house. The park, once the property of the Marquis of Bute, was given to the Inland Revenue and thus to the people of Cardiff in the 1940's as a way of paying inheritance tax. Max thought about his own comments the previous evening concerning the aristocracy losing property and thought how beneficial the process was of taking from the rich to help improve the life of the poorer, but it must have caused the poor Marquis pain. The park was beautiful and the tree lined walk gave the view ahead a formality which Max loved.

'Just think Simon, this was owned by one man,' Max reflected. 'Did you know that in 1892, a case was brought involving the son of the then Marquis of Bute. A fraud had taken place in the Cardiff Savings Bank and the Marquis's son had been appointed a director when only a few days old. He never turned up to work once in thirty eight years,' Max stated.

'Why not?, asked Simon with some curiosity although he was all too well aware that Max would often trip off on a tangent about something or another about which no-one else really cared.

'Well his father was one of the richest men on earth so I guess there was a familial disincentive,' Max chuckled. He continued. 'The case turned on whether the Marquis's son could be made liable for the loss as he was a director. The best person to sue in life is always the one who is the richest so it was an important case for both the Marquis and the issue of directors' duties.'

'What happened?' asked Simon.
'Well the courts concluded that as he had not actually turned up to work in thirty eight years he was not responsible for the fraud and thus he was not liable. Had he turned up once and not found out about the crime then he would have been.'
'So less is more then,' Simon offered. Max smiled.

'Perhaps, but don't you see, that would never happen today. Firstly, the concept of aristocracy. What are they actually ruling these days except their estates and so many of those are owned by the National Trust. This park, no longer a wealthy man's privilege but open to the public. The director today (Max's PhD had been on the topic of directors' duties yet he was kind enough to rarely mention it to his friends), he would never have been allowed to get away with it. Passivity is a breach of section 174 Companies Act 2006,' Max stated in an overly affected manner.

'Max where is your mind?' Simon enquired wearily.

'It's about change Simon,' Max continued uninhibited. 'So much has changed. Here I am today at forty two and going to marry a man. I am a man marrying a man, legally allowed by the Civil Partnership Act of 2004. Here we are walking through a park that one hundred years ago you could be prosecuted or even shot at by the game keeper if we walked through it.'

'You still can,' interrupted Simon, referencing the cruising area nearer town.

'Seriously Simon, it may be British and it may be incremental, but don't you feel privileged that with all this change we are afforded so much freedom? We have had a revolution in this country,' Max declared.' 'It just wasn't overnight.'

'The old library from the castle was sold a few years back,' Simon stated (not one to let his own knowledge base be kept under a bushel). 'It fetched over twenty million,' Simon started to sing in an overly affected baritone voice, 'Shall we here the room again singing the songs of angry men . . .'

'Oh shut up and go and live in sin,' Max snapped but with affection.

'Are you really happy Max? asked Simon.

'Yes I really am.' This time Max could not have been more sincere.

Chapter Three

'Cameron, we must tell my mother that we are getting married.' Max was shaving in the bathroom when he spoke while Cameron was in the adjoining dressing room undertaking the biggest task of the day; choosing a shirt. Between them they had acquired over one hundred and fifty and had purchased a new wardrobe which necessitated moving the actual bed into a room at the front of the house. Triple glazing had been installed as a result as the front room overlooked a busy road. The domino effect, Max had thought at the time; moving your partner in means moving your bed out. How ironic.

Cameron always looked immaculate. As he sifted through the Guccis, Armanis and Westwoods, Max felt that he could have rivalled Dok Wong or was it Kok Dong, in putting outfits together.

Max looked at Cameron as he emerged from the dressing room. The mirrored wardrobes replicating his slim figure and displaying a playful striped shirt from Mr Allesandrini, a designer from Rome who seemed to empathise with slim men who were so often disenfranchised by some designers who assumed that all men had bellies and required a tent like shirt to fit everything in. Max and Cameron had often shopped for shirts and would get excited at the fit of some beautiful garment on a manikin only to discover to their disappointment that the shirt was heavily pinned at the back and suitable for someone who had never visited a gym or who suffered with sever water retention.

Max and Cameron had met eighteen months prior after a short exchange of messages on a web site called Gaydar. Max, who had met several inappropriate individuals on the site was aware of its limitations and of the code involved in some of the self portraits. Rugby build meant rugby pitch build, slim meant plump. Toned meant not quite as plump but no muscle, muscled could mean just having a heart beat and bi-curious meant completely raving but shy about it.

They had met in a local wine bar overlooking the Bay. Max had arrived on time and Cameron was forty minutes late keeping Max on edge by text messages declaring a work issue had arisen. Max had waited calling Simon for company and declaring that this was probably going to be another cul de sac but when eventually Cameron arrived, Max heard his voice for the first time and he knew that this would be different. Cameron was every bit as beautiful as his pictures and within minutes the couple had realised that their expectations had been exceeded. The evening went into the small hours and the two arranged to meet on the Sunday when Max cooked lunch and they ate it outside in the garden. It was a beautiful day and everything was so effortless.

They courted for two weeks before they had slept together and for Max who had become sanitised to sex for quite some time, it was a realisation that making love still existed in the world. He was always concerned that Cameron enjoyed sex with him, always affectionate with him, always stayed close afterwards and always ensured that Cameron was fulfilled. To him, that was the best he knew how to be as a lover and from that, patience, kindness and trust had grown. It was an amazing development in Max's life and he felt a stronger man for it.

'When shall we go?' Cameron asked.

'Today, you never know we could be on the six o clock news,' Max joked. 'Imagine it, one of the oldest gays in the village has finally decided to settle down and marry. Dr Max Hubbard-White made the announcement after coming out of hospital where had just undergone a Joan Rivers make over rendering him speechless due to the botox. He signed to the waiting media that he was to wed his partner of eighteen months, Cameron Stewart by gesturing with his right hand that his penis was now only for one man.'

'Who was doing the news?' Cameron asked through fits of laughter.

'Fiona Bruce,' replied Max. 'She looked so disappointed.'

Howls of laughter came from the dressing room, so much so that Benson, their beloved Beagle dog started barking. Benson was a purchase Max and Cameron had made earlier that year after their pre wedding honeymoon in Paris and just after the anniversary of their first meeting. He, like Paris, was gorgeous and like all Beagles, quite impossible to train. He was tricolour, with eyes that could melt you at thirty paces. He stopped the village when Max went to the local Spar for cigarettes and the staff made a huge fuss of him. Max disappeared when he walked Benson. The dog was their baby and made their small and unassuming family complete. He was the focus of their attention and he loved them back so generously. Naughty, impossible, adorable, Benson had certainly been a wise purchase.

As Max raised himself out of the bath, Benson lunged forward making Max vulnerable. Max had seen what he could do to dog proof plastic toy and he wanted to ensure that he remained fully equipped for his civil partnership. Max dressed after pacifying Benson with a small flannel and gave Cameron a big hug.

'This will prove an interesting afternoon,' he said as Cameron snuggled into his neck and Benson jumped up at them, not wanting to be out of the affectionate moment.
'It will be fine I'm sure,' replied Cameron, 'I think your mother will be very happy for us.'

Two hours later, Max and Cameron placed the dog precariously into his cage (euphemistically called a cot), a gift from well equipped, dog owning, lesbian friends which was seated in the back of Max's car.

'Shall we have the roof off?' asked Cameron.

'It's a beautiful day, yes,' replied Max. The slow theatrical lifting of the roof brought with it a warmth from the sun that made Max feel more at ease with the imparting of their news. He breathed in and sighed.

As he turned off the M4 and up the A467 Max breathed more deeply. The hills were always a source of comfort for him. As a young man he had conquered most of them with a young friend called Aiden, a red haired youth who loved nice clothes, never had a girlfriend and who had played a Soft Cell record for Max once when they were alone together in Aiden's parents' house. How keen the family had been to point out several years later that Aiden was really happy with a lovely young girl called Denise and that he did not have much interest in hill walking any longer. Max had been surprised by this. He had no sexual attraction to Aiden, he just enjoyed hill walking and Aiden had been easy company. Still Max thought perhaps if he had had such guarding parents, would he have come out as a gay man? He then looked over at Cameron and sighed. What did it matter, he was happy and felt that at least he had been able to develop naturally. It made him focused somehow that there was nothing in him to hide. He was a conservative man in many ways but this had absolutely nothing to do with his sexuality.

'I love you,' Cameron said quite from nowhere.
'Love you more,' replied Max
'Oh I doubt it,' said Cameron.

Max's mother, Einwen, lived in a small cottage overlooking the most picturesque of fields and backed onto a forest. There was a small brook in front of the house and it was so quiet you could hear it babbling away giving the most restful of background noises. It was a small village called Hafodyrynys, meaning in welsh, island of the summer-house. The valley in which it lay was unusual in that it ran east west. This prompted all sorts of myths about shepherdesses haunting the mountain side and white ladies in pubs. It had expanded two years prior when a new 'luxury' estate was built on an old council wasteland. The village was no longer supported by a shop but contained a florists, a pub and a Chinese take-away. All the essentials, Max often thought.

Max's mother's family had been in the village since the time the census began. After his hill farming great grandfather, his grandfather had been a miner and married above his station to a shop owner's daughter. They had seven children and Max's mother was the youngest and only surviving daughter.

Einwen lived in one of the oldest parts of the village. Max had bought the house for her when he was twenty five and this had made him proud. The cottage had been built by Max's great grandfather together with three further cottages two of which were owned by other family members. It was so typical of Welsh valley life. You could get most of your family not just in the same town but in the same street.

He remembered when he bought the cottage, which led to some farms and a dead end on top of the hill, his aunt had lived in the house two doors down. His Aunt Jayne a woman that was both his aunt and his second cousin (so Texan) had declared, 'Love, are you sure its wise buying the place, the road outside is so busy these days. Do you know four cars went past today,' she declared with a righteous indignation in her voice.

'Really?' Max had replied, 'Four?'

'Yes,' Jayne replied, 'two went up and two came back down again, it was like Piccadilly Circus.'

Max reflected on a statue of Eros being placed in the middle of the field opposite and he imagined two cars tooting at fifteen miles an hour while his beloved aunt was ooohing and aahing in her home. How commuters in London would think it heaven to have such congestion.

'Oh I think Mum will cope,' Max had said with as much constructiveness in his voice as he could muster.

The cottages were part of the village's history. Max's great-grandfather loved building and purchasing property and had acquired quite a collection by the time he died. As a result, his son and daughter-in-law had been able to provide all of their children with a home, which had prompted Aunty Jayne to enquire when Max had bought his house, 'I understand you are using a mortgage to purchase the house for your mother.'

'Yes aunt,' Max replied.

'Your uncle and I used a solicitor,' she stated with matter of fact authority.

'Thanks,' Max had said, 'I think I'll do the same.' Jayne had beamed believing she had made an important contribution to the proceedings.

As Max drove up to the cottages, he was mindful of the way meetings with his mother could go. Forget the irregular verb, this woman, armed with a third lung which made her capable of talking for twenty minutes without drawing breath, had mastered the art of the irregular conversation. You had to think two minutes ahead just to ensure continuity. She was a strong woman with very dedicated views on womanhood. She believed that a woman's place was to support her family and that in return this meant that unmitigated respect should follow from that family. The problem with this thesis was that she had married Max's father. George White. He had been the youngest of two sons, born into a marriage that was the product of a shot gun wedding. He was ten years younger than his elder brother and was adored, often to the exclusion of the elder brother, by his parents.

Max saw the pain still in his mother's face which was a product of George White's belief that if he wasn't made happy in life then he was the immediate victim of circumstance. He would often take this out on Einwen physically but her philosophy on commitment and marriage meant that she had endured eighteen years of marriage to him until his own mother died and he had immediately filed for divorce. How odd it is that such a weak man could show physical strength and forge another marriage with a woman (his second wife) with whom he had lived for at least ten years and on whom he had cheated, whereas a woman of strong principles could be left so hurt and remote. Max's parents had fashioned his views of marriage and relationships and he knew that it took two strong people to make a marriage work and if he ever married he would look for strength first. He had found that in Cameron as well as loyalty. Max hurt for his mother whom he loved and of whom he despaired.

The door opened as he and Max got out decamping Benson from his cage.

'Hello love,' Einwen said with that slightly singing lilt that Max and so many of his friends had striven consciously to overcome.

'Hi Mum,' Max said with a kiss on the cheek.
Cameron and Einwen exchanged embraces before the attention was turned to Benson.

'Oh he's gorgeous, and growing, yes you are growing aren't you, yes you are yes you are.' Einwen loved Benson. Who wouldn't?

Benson lapping up the attention literally running straight into the kitchen where some dog food had been placed in a bowl.

'Mum what food is this, I'm very strict about what he eats,' said Max with some urgency in his voice and a frown.

'Oh it's fine love, the dog it belonged to died,' Einwen beamed as she said this.

'Died!' bleated Max.

'Yes, I knew you had Benson so I asked the owner to give it to me rather than let it go to waste. It's such a shame going to waste,' Einwen declared with a practical tone in her voice which expressed a lifetime of thrift.

'To be clear Mum, the dog's death wasn't connected to the food?' Max enquired confident that it wasn't but just to be sure that his mother's money saving measures were not going to result in another canine fatality.

'No, he got run down chasing a sheep,' said Einwen with a truly noticeable element of sorrow in her voice.

'Yes the road through the village is so busy Mum I'm glad you live so far away from it,' said Max.

'No love he got run down by the sheep. I think they thought well he's only small so they ganged up on him.' Einwen's sincerity was earnest yet Max had to muffle a giggle.

'So are you ok Mum?' Max said, reigning in the conversation which had taken years of practise.

'I am' she said, 'you and Cameron look well. I saw your grandmother today.'

'What!' exclaimed Max, 'Granny Hubbard?'

'Yes,' Einwen declared with a tone that suggested Max had somehow lost the plot.

'Mum, she died thirty three years ago,' Max offered gently.

'It's thirty two actually,' declared Einwen with some indignation. Max thought for a moment, as the spirit of Bea Arthur ran through him and he thought it time to consider a maximum security Shady Pines nursing home. Instead he enquired, 'So how is she?'

'Oh she's fine,' Einwen declared with a child's peace of mind on her face. Max continued, 'So how is . . . she looking?' As he said this he looked at Cameron who had the oddest expression on his face sensing that this child had no such peace.

'Well it wasn't her in person,' she said with such a phlegmatic air in her voice that it made Max feel that he should be admonished for doubting her grasp on reality. 'She came in the form of a butterfly,' Max's doubts were immediately restored.

'She came in and I knew it was her, she flew around for a while then left. I think it's a good sign,' Einwen declared happily.

'I have no doubt,' Max lied and took a long sip of the tea that had been provided. Right he thought, that's a great conduit into our news.

'Mum, I have news,' Max declared with an excitement in his voice.

'You're getting married,' Einwen responded with a big grin on her face.

'Yes,' Max said with a winded look on his face. His mother was always very good at being able to take away his cake. He remembered once buying her a car for her birthday. Upon delivering it, he walked into the cottage with a big grin on his face and his mother had burst into tears. Ah, he had thought, she's overwhelmed. It had transpired that her cat of seventeen years had died the night before rendering her inconsolable for at least two weeks. Max had hated that cat. He often thought as it came into the room that it secretly smoked pot upstairs and would look at Max as if to declare, what the hell are you doing here. It also looked like Peggy Lee, in her later years.

'So how did you know?' enquired Max, still deflated.

'Well I told you, your grandmother came and I knew there was good news coming.' Einwen's tone was convincing. 'I think it's lovely, I'm very happy for you both.' With that, Einwen gave Cameron a big hug and kiss. 'You will look after him won't you?' Einwen asked Cameron.

'Oh yes I will,' Cameron replied. Max gulped and his eyes watered slightly.

It later transpired that Aunty Jayne had let slip to Einwen that Max and Cameron were to marry. Jayne now lived in sheltered accommodation but was in regular touch with Einwen. Her husband, Uncle Powell had recently died. Max and Cameron had visited him in hospital shortly before this and the old man, riddled with infection, remained a consummate gentleman to the end. Max had adored him as a child and this had remained. He had been so pleased to meet Cameron and Max had felt how important it was that someone so closely connected with his family's past generations had given his approval. Max had cried like a small child when they had left the hospital and went straight to see his aunt upon his uncle's strictest instructions. It was like having a father in his life and Max loved that and him. It was there that they had told Aunty Jayne about the wedding and she swore to secrecy. Max knew that that would be far too much to ask.

Max looked at his mother. She was smiling and there was a flushed look on her face. Max anticipated a barrage of questions about dates and venues but instead the conversation reverted to his beautiful niece, Poppy.

'Poppy's ballet classes are going well,' Einwen said. 'She's a natural dancer and her teacher is very pleased with her progress,' Einwen declared proudly.
'That's great Mum,' Max was sincere. 'It's in the blood.'

Einwen had been a ballet dancer and contortionist as a child and possessed some unbelievable pictures of her with her chest on the floor and her feet next to them. She had remained painfully slim until she married George White. The unhappy marriage was nowhere detected on Einwen's face when she spoke about her grand daughter for whom she took far too much responsibility. How different she was to Marianne, thought Max, different perhaps but every bit as strong if not stronger.

Then of course there was Max himself. In 1983, he was the British Junior Sequence Old Time ballroom dancing champion, and was still in possession of some equally remarkable photographs as evidence. The Tower Ballroom in Blackpool had been the scene of many successes for

Max as a child and he thought now how lucky he had been that his mother had encouraged him to dance. It was a skill, the discipline of which had translated into many other aspects of his life as a man. His childhood had been a parallel universe to that of the other children in the village. School then dance class. He had been good, but the idea of a working class boy in the Welsh valleys doing ballroom dancing had rendered him peculiar and probably gay in the opinion of most if not all of his contemporaries.

Max had stopped ballroom dancing upon attending university to read law, but there were times, watching Strictly Ballroom or visiting Preston, only seventeen miles from the Blackpool Mecca, on business, that he reflected upon his childhood; the bitching, the practise, the bitching, the travelling, the bitching, the politics. Max chuckled. It seemed that so much of life was wasted in making negative comments about others and what really was the prize? Some trophies that got dusty and memories, yes nice memories but nevertheless now quite intangible.

Max felt a little hurt by the lack of questions from his mother, but let it pass as instalment by instalment of

Poppy's week was delivered with great detail. Max began to whither and wished he had a scotch in front of him. After a while, he stood.

'Well mum, must go, things to do, people to see.' He looked at Cameron and his partner who was always so sympathetic, put Benson's lead on him. They left shortly afterwards.

Once in the car, and warmed by the heated seats, Max asked Cameron, 'Do you really think she's happy about it?'

'Yes she seemed to be,' Cameron confirmed but with some hesitation.

'Yes I think it's more a case of she'd like to be don't you?' Max continued.

'What do you mean?' asked Cameron.

'Good parents want what they think is best for their children. Yet often there is a big expectation gap between the parent's wish and the child's actions. Yes the parent will be happy for the child if they are happy, but that doesn't mean that there is still an element of disappointment in the parent. I think my mother would have loved me to declare that I was marrying a woman and that she would have more than one grand child, but she has accepted the reality even though it falls short of her own hopes. She didn't even ask questions about the wedding,' Max said.

'Yes I noticed that,' replied Cameron. 'Perhaps she just doesn't want to pry.'

'Yes but parents are meant to pry, especially mothers, that's what they do, much to the annoyance of the children. I wanted her to pry,' declared Max.

'Now whose expectations are being thwarted?' Cameron said with a smile on his face.

'Ah ah, you got me there. Yes you may be right, perhaps she is being a better parent than I am crediting her, but I'm still disappointed. I wanted her to be like Diane Keaton in 'The Family Stone.' She would have asked questions.' Max and Cameron drove along for a while in silence.

'I know she loves me,' Max declared.

'Of course she loves you darling and so do I, very much,' replied Cameron. He always knew how to make Max feel so much better about everything.

'When I had coffee with Simon yesterday, we met Marianne, Charlotte's mother,' Max said.

'Yes you mentioned. Have you done anything about Basil?' Cameron teased.

'Yes we are going foxtrotting tonight in Metro's nightclub,' joked Max. He continued, 'She asked me if I was really happy. Do you think that everyone who isn't can't believe that other people are or that they think that I'm going to somehow change and not care about them any longer?' Max asked.

'I think someone might be getting anxious about the wedding and is a little over sensitive about people's comments,' Cameron stroked the back of Max's head and Max, like Peggy Lee, the cat, tilted his head into it. They continued to drive home, the hills black against the dark blue sky. Max felt calmer but there was still a nagging doubt about that afternoon. He looked across at Cameron and knew, arrogantly knew, that this was the right thing to do. He loved his partner very much.

Chapter Four

Work was at the core of Max's life, yet his friends had concluded that as he rarely mentioned it he was not Herculean in his work ethic. He would happily play along with this idea. Simon once called him in work stating, 'You're in work. What a surprise! I'm amazed you found the way there.' 'I have sat-nav,' Max had joked in his best Oscar Wilde mimic. The two had laughed about it at the time, but Max was a little hurt. He loathed those people who talked endlessly about their jobs at the expense of any real communication about the person to whom they were talking. It was just bad manners. In any event, what would there be to talk about, he wondered as he sat in his large office which he shared with two other colleagues, Gwylim and Tina, both lecturers as he. He liked them.

He couldn't imagine his friends being curious about the formation principles of an express private trust, the recent changes in the rule against perpetuities not to mention the codification of directors' duties initiated by the Companies Act 2006, a remarkable achievement and one that Max had recommended in the conclusion of his own doctoral thesis in 1998 to no significant academic applause. No he was sure that his friends would wane at the idea of Max talking about his work so he kept his thoughts private.

Today he was in the office alone, preparing for another round of 'My subject is running beautifully and I'm the best lecturer in the University' meeting. Every year, the department in which he worked would gather together to discuss their modules and how they had run that year. Externals were involved but the crux was the students' marks. It had not been a classic year at the University of Abercwmsquiff, but it had not been a bad one either for his students. Max taught Trust Law to the final year and he couldn't help wondering if some of them turned up to see what jacket he was wearing, or just to get out of the cold. Some of the papers belied any contact with academic curiosity or indeed a book, the latter becoming increasingly marginalised in modern education, thanks to internet searches.

Once Max had asked an HND (Higher National Diploma) student to read from a case evaluation. She had expressed that the whole idea of political reasons for raising the corporate veil was a 'vargoo con kept' which Max realised instantly translated into 'vague concept' in the more traditional english. Higher education was meant to be inclusive but there were limits.

Max was old fashioned in his attitude to teaching. He had once commented to a shocked meeting of the department that the use of computers in the classroom (power point he thought it was called or was that a porn movie?) contributed nothing to the intellectual substance of the lecture and detracted from the in put of the lecturer himself. Max made his lectures entertaining but clear. His job was to communicate knowledge in a way that could best be understood by his students and to this end the hourly audiences pivoted entirely on him. Two things were essential, you had to be up to date and you had to make it relevant. Not easy tasks but Max always enjoyed the challenge. He was after all a lecturer, not an academic administrator or a manager but a lecturer and to that end he was totally committed to his work.

He would always start his course by asking his class if they had any middle class grandparents that lived in north Cardiff or perhaps the Vale, who were wealthy. This would result in ears being pricked up by those students who possessed such an asset and a look of glumness from those who didn't. 'Well,' Max would continue, 'if you have this subject is for you. Go home tonight and ask them would they like to be taxed upon death giving forty per cent of their wealth over seven hundred thousand to the tax man or would they rather set up a trust for their accomplished grandchild who is doing so well at university.' Giggles would be heard around the room. 'Don't be tacky about it though, take some flowers with you. Lillies I think just to send home the message.' More respectful giggles ensued and Max often felt that they either liked him at that point or thought him affectionately mad. Mmm Mad Max, well it wouldn't be the first, he thought.

Like any lecturer, Max loved questions and feed back and he loved reading exam scripts where it was clearly evident that the student had actually listened in the classroom. It would literally make him well with tears as an evaluation of the implied trust was made by a young man or woman and how the effects of co-habitation increased the number of occasions when such a trust was applied for in court.

This morning's meeting though was a big affair. Coffee and sandwiches had been ordered to a 'level two' standard. This was marginally above level one, and included tomato and parsley as garnish (level one was just parsley) and meat! 'Level one' sandwiches would contain something that looked like meat but the Food Standards Agency had never had the stomach to make a transparent verdict on the subject. The level two sandwiches were served with tea or coffee, one of those self assembly situations which caused queuing, or bottled water. The department and the externals sat.

The meeting was chaired by Rupert, a man a little older than Max who was the department's quality guru. This was not a flippant observation made by Max. If there was a problem in the department, Rupert would be the person to whom Max would turn and he always gave such constructive advice. Rupert was a tall man, married with children, won awards for teaching and knew everything about university procedures and processes, two words Max loathed. Max liked him.

'Before we start today,' Rupert began, 'I would like to offer my congratulations to Max.'

Max froze in his seat. Had he been promoted to Professor on the basis of writing only one article that year? No, that would require at least two. He waited.

'We understand Max that you are getting married in August. On behalf of the department I wanted to wish you all the best in your nuptials.' Max reflected upon that idea for a moment prepared to smirk but then realising that Rupert's complete lack of base wit precluded any such response.

Max was dumfounded. How on earth? Had the news really got a hold of the story and Ms Bruce suicidal now at home with a bottle of gin? Ah, no, it was Glenda, the department's long standing secretary and in whom Max confided most things. She had undertaken her usual communication briefings about everyone to everyone. Max felt a little vulnerable as he sat there amongst his colleagues. It's not that he was shy about his sexuality but he was private. He never liked men kissing in public or even holding hands but he was value neutral in his prejudice because he didn't like straight couples doing it either. Intimacy implied discretion and if it didn't it should, he would reflect.

As he thought about this there followed a liberal splattering of congratulations from some of his colleagues and surprisingly some confused looks. Max thought he should clarify.

'Thank you Rupert, I'm not sure I can call it a marriage, it's a civil partnership.' Relief on the faces of the confused. 'Yes I'm off the shelf at last and for once not walking up the shopping aisle.' A tame joke but Max was truly nervous about people's reaction. He had always been robust when responding to any prejudice. He remembered a comeback some months prior when a man had shouted homophobic abuse outside a gay public house.

'Want to suck my cock faggot?' the young gentleman had yelled.

'Thank you,' Max had responded, 'but like a lot of British people I don't floss.' The young man's friends looked perplexed and had walked away thanks to the presence of two police officers but Max had felt ready for a confrontation. No this was different. Max knew that even in higher education an outwardly intellectual acceptance of homosexuality was a façade and experiencing prejudice and the eventual feeling of remoteness were commonplace among gay men.

As the meeting progressed, each academic remained measured but robust about how well their own subject had been taught. Well you're not going to say you were dreadful, Max thought. The marks were studied closely and adjustments made where the externals felt that a cohort had been treated too harshly or that some unfortunate student qualified for mitigation due to the demise of a close relative. It was interesting but some students seemed to develop a very extended family often having three or four grandmothers all passing away within their final two years at university. *To loose one grandmother . . .* Max thought.

When the proceedings eventually came to an end after five hours, and the comments had been made by the externals about how well everything was and how a few adjustments could be made here and there, Max felt his arm grabbed by his colleague and friend, Marie. Marie was someone Max always looked forward to seeing and a chance meeting in the corridor always resulted in a long exchange of questions into their respective families and loved ones. Like Max she had been a dancer in her youth and remained slim and elegant. She worked incredibly hard and had placed herself in a position where she worked part time in order to be a full time mother. This Max thought, was the ultimate in emancipation as it reflected the freedom of choice. Her grace and determination to be good at everything she did was an inspiration for Max and she and her husband were a willowy and handsome couple. They were also Christians, but the very best sort.

'Max, that's wonderful news,' she said excitedly and it was so meant. They smiled at each other for a while. Her husband was also called Cameron and Max responded to questions on the big day; where was it going to be, the reception, the guest list. All normal things about an event that Max thought would be considered odd by so many and evil by others. Here he was though with a charming, well educated woman who was without mitigation pleased for him. He smiled inwardly. He had once heard that people concentrate on the negative up to three times that of the positive. Why was that? He looked at his friend and they had a small and awkward embrace as others began to gather around, the older men, being respectful and smiling, making comments about their marriage, oh and children, while some of his female colleagues actually gave him a kiss. Max was happy to feel so accepted. Perhaps it was he who was a little reticent with people and thus he expected others to feel the same way but that was fine, that was his age, his background and his manner and at least it appeared there was an acceptance of that here.

On his way home that evening, Max's mind was reflective. Robert had died four years prior and it had been tough. He remembered the night Robert died. It was a Thursday and Max had been writing Christmas cards. He knew Robert was ill and had only found out the extent of his Parkinsons months before Robert's death. Robert was a lot older than Max. They had known each other for twenty years. The relationship had started as friends but Robert had made it clear that he wanted more and Max being a young man of twenty had about him all the usual vanities which precluded any reciprocity.

They were both doctors. Max of law of course and Robert of chemistry. Robert had been awarded a CVO for his assistance in the Investiture of the Prince of Wales in 1969 and was a proud royalist, which was unusual for a first language Welsh speaker. They had both had King Charles spaniels before they met. Quite by coincidence, Robert's little dog had been called Admiral, while Max's had been Nelson. Robert had over the years become

Max's life, and his rock. His death was a devastating blow for Max's emotional security.

Their relationship had evolved. Love making was always a distant affair but sincere and respectful. Max gave what he could out of love for his older partner, Robert gratefully received but conscious of the limitations which Max knew hurt him. Together though they had found a mutual comfort and strength and the night before Robert died Max had asked him, 'Do you love me?' Robert had answered, 'Yes very much.' Max knew this was important as Robert's usual response was, 'Oh just a little bit.'

Max had seen the decline of his former partner over a two year period, the baking of cakes had stopped, the driving of the car had lessened and after an accident involving a misjudged turn, Max had demanded that Robert sell the car, much to the vocal remonstrations of his late partner. Max had sorted out the subsequent insurance claim and saw his elderly partner cry.

'I used to run an important government department!' sobbed Robert,' and now I cant even sort out this.'

Max knew Robert was dying when he visited his doctor with Robert and the doctor seemed to think that Max had been uncaring for not knowing for sure about the Parkinsons but Robert was so secretive about it.

Towards the end, caring for Robert had become a full time experience, which almost broke Max although Max would never admit it to his friends. He bathed Robert every day, made food, organised the doctor and ensured that Robert was as comfortable as possible for which Robert had been grateful. How disciplined one has to be and how removed, when you cease being a lover and friend and have to take on the role of carer.

The night of Robert's death Max had gone upstairs to check that Robert was asleep. He wasn't.

'Max,' he began, 'did the doctor give you anything for me?' he asked.

'Yes Robert,' Max replied, 'he said you were to have sex, drugs or rock 'n roll. So take your pick 'coz its getting late.' Max's flippancy was a coping method seeing his partner of thirteen years go from being a robust and feared senior civil servant to a man that could no longer drive his own car. The doctor had been called twice that day with Robert moaning that Max was guilty of over care.

'Who's the prime minister?' Max asked.

'Lloyd bloody George,' replied Robert. Max was pleased with the answer as Robert's sense of wit had remained. Max loved him very much for that and had laughed uncontrollably that day as Max tried to hold a tube under Robert's penis in order to extract urine for tests.

'What awful situations one finds oneself in,' he had declared with his usual lofty tone.

'You wait 'til you see what going back in,' replied Max, and they laughed so much so that Robert gave an unscheduled squirt and the task was complete. Max had held his hand and Robert sighed.

That evening Robert looked tired. 'I'd like to go to the bathroom,' he said and as his walking was now very unsteady, Max stood behind him and guided him into the next room. Max sang as he did this, 'Me and my shadow . . .' Robert had laughed out loud. Max had sat his partner down. That moment, Robert's head had rolled backwards and his eyes seemed to roll with it. He made the most gruesome of guttural sounds and fell into Max's arms. Max held him up but knew Robert was slipping away instantly. He grabbed his mobile phone which he had placed on the window sill and called 999. The lady on the phone asked for which service and Max responded by stating that his partner was having a heart attack and was turning blue. The woman, well trained and very calm, asked for the address and talked Max through the resuscitation procedure. Robert seemed to respond to this and Max with tears clouding his vision, heard the door bell. He had to leave Robert on the bathroom floor while he ran downstairs. The paramedics came in and took one look at Robert.

'Your father's dead sir,' he declared. 'He's been dead for a while.'
'No!' Max barked, he was fine five minutes ago. He can't be dead.'

The paramedics looked at each other and while apparatus was brought in to recover Robert. Max was guided out of the room by the third paramedic and sat on the stairs for what seemed like an age. After only forty five minutes, with voices saying he's responding, the paramedic who had confidently declared Robert as dead, came out and told Max that this could now be confirmed. Max froze, his shoulders became erect and suddenly he felt much older. Robert had left him. After the paramedics had left and the police were called, Max went back into the bathroom.

Robert's eyes were still open. Max gently closed them and his tears fell uncontrollably on to Robert's face which was less blue but pasty. He asked Robert to forgive him for not being the lover he had really wanted. He sat by the side of his life partner and stared at the towels opposite. Max had never felt so thwarted and so alone. Robert had been the silent force in Max's life and had been a measuring influence on Max. Max was now alone.

Max was still crying four years on as he sat in his car on the A470, the main road home from Abercwmsquiff to Cardiff. He had learned to keep his speed at a steady sixty five as he wiped his eyes with the back of his hand. The parade of white lights coming toward him and the procession of red in front of him were sparkling. Was it so disrespectful to Cameron, that he should still feel so upset about loosing Robert and after all this time? No, it was the fact that he, a middle aged, middle class man, unassuming and private, had had the privilege of being with Robert the moment God had taken him back. Yes Max's thoughts turned to how some experiences in life were like beacons that shone out to you at moments of fear or anguish but also moments of joy and happiness. Robert's death was the strongest light in his hopes in this respect. Max's love for Robert had taught him that there had been a life that he had loved, not with the fresh passion of a young man, but with the maturity and respect of a grown up. He had realised how much he had needed Robert and how much Robert had loved him. It was more powerful than money or sex, and seeing his late partner enter mortality had made him prepared at last to be able to commit to someone else. His mind turned straight away to Cameron.

It was evening when he got in and Max was met by a very excited Benson, who had ripped apart another dog proof toy from Tesco. Max smiled at him as the tricolour beauty licked Max's face and ear. Cameron was in the kitchen looking very smart and cooking something wonderful. He had the silliest of grins on his face.

'Hello darling,' Max said.
No response but a big grin remained on Cameron's face.
'What's wrong with you?' Max asked the smiling becoming infectious.
'I'm going to be on the telly,' Cameron declared. Not since Cheri Blair contracted lock jaw was there a smile so broad.
'Oh,' commented Max, 'your own chat show?'

'Oh it will be,' declared Cameron, 'I've been chosen as a contestant on 'Come Dine With Me.'

'That's wonderful news,' said Max, trying to sound enthusiastic and thinking well at least it's not 'Four Weddings'. He was confident of his own demise and thus funeral if that had been Cameron's news.

'When is it?' Max enquired.

'Six weeks time,' replied Cameron.

'Six weeks!' exclaimed Max, 'but we're getting married in three months, won't that be invasive?'

'No,' assured Cameron, slightly hurt by the mitigation in Max's enthusiasm. 'I will take care of everything and you won't have to be involved.'

Max smiled at his partner. Strangers from the television entering his well researched abode and he not involved. Quite an esoteric evaluation! He thought that married life would be about making his partner feel good and being supportive but this was going to be a real test. Strangers coming and making judgements was not something about which Max felt at ease. Still, at least filming would only be for one day at their home and Max checked that the crew was insured for damage to the property if not for the damaging effect on any self respect Max might endure.

Timothy Brown

'Well let's have a toast then,' Max announced with an outward show of bravado and several text messages were sent out to friends with the ostensibly good news. 'Champagne?'

'I have a bottle chilling,' replied Cameron.

'What will you be cooking my little Nigel Slater?' asked Max. Cameron and Max actually enjoyed Mr Slater's performances on the TV as his recipes always seemed accessible. Max had never tried one but he felt he could if he had wanted to.

'I thought I won't compromise,' replied Cameron, 'I'm doing rabbit and pheasant for the main course.'

'Won't that disenfranchise people, bunnies on your plate and all that. People are very odd about meat darling. Look at the French.' Max smiled as he said this. 'They mock us for our roast beef, yet they eat horse. Just think eating poor dapple who ends up in a dapple au vin or something. I think you may have issues there my love. I've watched the programme once and the people on there didn't strike me as being connoisseurs.

'Well it's a competition and I'm going to make what I think is good food.' Cameron was determined and Max admired him for this in spite of his reservations. Cameron was nothing if not an accomplished cook. Max had been pleasantly surprised that this had come as part of a very well groomed package, a very slim figure and a radiant smile. He looked at Cameron while he busied in the kitchen.

'Have they told you who the other contestants are?' enquired Max, almost with a pencil in his hand making an inventory of the silver and china in the dining room.

'There's a self made millionaire I think, a woman with breast enhancements and a property land lady,' replied Cameron

'Well they seem safe unless one of the breasts explodes,' replied Max.

Cameron looked at him with a 'stop worrying and just enjoy it' look on his face. Max retreated to the sitting room.

Benson at this point had literally pulled all the stuffing out of the toy dog which now resembled road kill. The green foam littered the gallery around his cot as the smell of dinner wafted through into the dining room. This was domestic life in a way Max could never have imagined. His thoughts today remained private not wishing to mitigate Cameron's joy. He loved his family. He was looking forward to being Cameron's civil partner.

Chapter Five

Max woke early the following morning. It was five O'clock and mindful of the Hassidic Jewish notion that the sinners of the night were now in bed, while the sinners of the day were still there, he woke with a sense of aloneness. He loved Cameron very much and he was such a source of strength for him but a reality TV show in his well researched abode filled him with a sense of exposure. He thought of all those past imperfect lovers that might be tuning in to Channel Four, pens at the ready waiting to expose his now comfortable life as a façade for the nefarious adventures Max had explored in his youth. Cameron was fast asleep next to him and he wondered at his partner's ability to sleep. Six hours was more than enough and he assumed that Cameron was sleeping off 2002-2009, when they met.

Max thought how odd it was that when he was awake in the house and everyone else was asleep how like a trespasser he felt as though he had started a day in a family that hadn't woken to give the picture its full meaning. He crept about in the dressing room even though Cameron slept for Russia and several of the Balkan states. His mind was still probably as far away as they.

Max went downstairs and immediately started his habitual cleaning routine. Staff was now out of the question due to financial constraints but he didn't mind as it made him feel at one with God. Cleanliness was probably the best contribution Max could make to heaven and the spirit of Kim and Aggie was upon him. He was conscious that while he loved Benson, it was a responsibility that his home was kept free of any dog odour and that it was always presentable for a potential buyer. Such were the pains of having a mortgage. He remembered his aunt Jayne, who had made such a ruthless evaluation of traffic increase near his cottage asking him what a mortgage actually meant. He tried to explain but to her the idea of borrowing money to purchase a house seemed very irresponsible. Oh the joy of inheritance.

He worked methodically for over two hours before it became time to put on wellies and take Benson for his walk. The little Beagle who had yelped a few evaluations of disdain on being ignored in favour of the mop, jumped in anticipation and stretched as he came from his cot. If only you knew daddy's concerns, Max thought as the dog rather invasively sniffed between Max's legs and then started licking his hand. As Max grabbed the lead, the Beagle, like a lord of the manor stretched out on the kitchen floor and yawned as if to say, it's that time again, could you just wait for me to get myself together. Max had half expected to come home from work one day and see the beloved Benson sat in the chair with The Times and a sherry pondering over the middle east and declaring to Max, 'I don't think hate breeds love Max, have you seen what they're doing to the Palestinians, just taking their land. It's Poland all over again.'

While out walking, the sun gloriously set in the sky with its anticipatory warmth and parental comfort, Max thought about the next few weeks. Robert was now gone. His life had been much changed by that and he felt that the script of his life was being re written. Cameron was a strong man and Max admired that but what if he was so different to him. Lady Bracknell had scoffed at the idea of long engagements on the basis that they resulted in the couple finding out too much about each other before they married, but Max somehow saw that as a point in reverse psychology. Yes it was important to know someone before you married them but surely marriage played an important role in motivating a couple to make the effort to harmonize, otherwise people would not get married until they were almost dead. Marriage was not the objective but a conduit.

He threw a stick for Benson who seemed very non plused about chasing it, preferring instead to snuffle out an old turd that was under a park bench. Max thought as he took out his scented 'doggy doo' bags how irresponsible people were with their property and how pious he felt that in cleaning up someone else's responsibility made him feel like one of the local elders in the aged Llandaff. He had seen the masses out with their mongrels, allowing them to poo anywhere and everywhere without a care and full of 'well it's my council tax that pays for the maintenance so my dog has the right to poo anywhere' brigade. Yes, Max had thought and it's a seventy pound fine. I have an i-phone 4 and I'll take that smug look off your face with my evidence. Max toyed with the idea of gun control, and it's limitations but only briefly. The European

Convention on Human Rights and a trip to Alabama brought him back to the European fold of liberalism and sensitivity: but how he loathed those people.

The park was a beautiful asset opposite his home. Benson loved it, Max loved it, and after 9.00 pm quite a few gentlemen of learned conversation loved it, although for Max, that particular tete a tete was over. It was a notorious environment further to the centre of town that had provided many a tale around the dinner table in Max's youth. The apres club festivities, he had declared it to a friend. That was now years ago. The last time Max had experienced any such nocturnal encounters was on his way to the France v Wales rugby match. It had been controversially played on a Friday night, and Max had walked to the Millenium Stadium. Near the new bridge he had stopped to light up a cigarette after the new smoking ban precluded him from taking solace in the stadium. Perhaps the roof was too low, he thought. A young man approached him and said, 'There's nothing like a good fag mate,' and smiled knowingly.

'Oh yes there is,' replied Max, 'a good wank and I suggest you have one.' Max retreated quickly to the safety of the stadium leaving the young stranger with a peeved look on his face and a slight scoffing in his voice.

He walked back to the house and thought about his London friends. Gerard who was a producer on a travel programme, Marcus, who produced a children's channel and Dr Charles, who was an eminent cancer specialist in Harley Street. He hadn't told them about the great announcement, which Max felt sure was not the 'Come Dine With Me' experience and on arriving home he sent three identical messages to the Londoners. He waited for their reply.

Max was familiar with the importance of living in London. You could be a janitor in McDonalds in London but if you were a valleys boy it meant that you had moved away and were something special. How prescriptive success is for some people. You could be a perfectly good teacher in the Welsh valleys and be considered an under achiever, but if you went to London, you only had to see Annie Lennox once in the street and you were deemed interesting.

His friends had done a lot more than that and Max admired their achievement. He identified with them in one major respect, regardless of any relationship they encountered, whether a committed closed 'marriage', friendship or brief encounter, they all knew that the importance of remaining independent was paramount. The structures of family life, so much the province of heterosexual marriage, the wedding, children etc were not the norm for gay men. They could remain alone forever even when in love. Max wasn't always at ease with their attitude to life but he understood it and bore it in mind. His friends were amusing though. At dinner their contribution to the constitutional development of the UK had often included London succeeding from the Union on the basis of gay social advancement. Gerard was a particular advocate but also the keenest to loose his Welsh valleys roots regardless of the strength Max knew they gave him. Max had always played devil's advocate with Gerard's sentiments. He was an inhabitant of Islington, London, a place where he had lived for over twenty years.

'Go on then,' Max had riled at Gerard, 'wait 'til you need fresh lamb and soft water, we'll tax you 'til you have to move south of the River Thames.' Gerard had laughed out loud at this but it actually made him think about the prospect and downed a very large G and T.

The first message of congratulation came from Marcus. It was charming but perfunctory. Max had been on holiday with Marcus and Gerard shortly after Robert's death and Max had still not been forgiven by Marcus for a young Oklahoman man, rejecting Marcus in favour of the attentions of Max. Max smiled, the effort in manners was almost overwhelming. Max had been a good friend to Marcus. When his father died he had left his home divided between Marcus and his mother. Their solicitor had advised Marcus to transfer the house into Marcus's mother's name. Max had advised him that if his mother needed nursing care the house would be liable for the payments and would need to be sold but if he owned half of it, then the house could be protected. Two years later Marcus's mother went into care due to Alzheimer's and had stayed there for three years. This would have cost nearly one hundred thousand pounds yet due to Max's advice, the house was held jointly and remained an asset for Marcus when his mother sadly died. No thanks had ever been received for this and Max wondered about the entitlement issues that came with power in the media.

Max enjoyed them coming for trips but was made to feel by Gerard that it was a far greater privilege for Max than Max perceived. Gerard's own living space was a garden flat in Islington that after four years had thick brown paper as flooring.

'This will never catch on,' Max had stated after one of his overnight stays. A week end was out of the question because of the damp and Max's asthma.

'I know,' Gerard had replied with a sense of resignation, 'but you see it's finding the time. It's such hard work what with the television channel and everything.'

Max smiled, this was the statutory response from Gerard whenever a hint of criticism of him was offered.

Next came Dr Charles. If God had created a more charming and well educated man, Max wondered where. Charles had been the partner of a media type for eight years. Billy was the grandson of Texan oil baron and Charles the son of good working class stock. Charles personified wisdom and social movement in a way that made Max feel humbled. He had more letters after his name than in it, and every time he stayed with Max, a bottle of single malt, or a bouquet of flowers were always close behind on his departure. Max loved Charles and often wondered why he had no feelings for him other than friendship. Max's conclusion was that he loved him so much as a friend that it would only end in something detrimental if further exploration was enacted. Oh and yes, Charles loved his partner.

The message from Charles read simply. 'Max, I am overjoyed at the news. I send my best wishes to you and Cameron, it's no more than you deserve. Love Charles.'

Max breathed out. He was contented that even though it wasn't a call, it was a quick and sincere text. Max knew Charles. When Max was thirty, Charles who had taken a gap year to work in IT at Buckingham Palace, had sent Max a message from Buck House wishing him a happy birthday. How it mitigated the sense of middle agedom for Max and of course made Robert both proud and highly suspicious about the Royal household's employees misusing their position not to mention paper. Robert was always the civil servant, Max had thought.

The call from Gerard came at 10.15am and Gerard sounded as though Max had woken him with the text message. Obviously a school night, thought Max.

'Hi love,' Gerard had started lightly, but not fooling Max for a moment as to the potential remit for both evaluation and judgement from one of his oldest friends.

'Got your text, yes that's great news. You OK?' His voice sounded like Marlene Dietrich had just swallowed some Just Brazils only to discover that she had a nut allergy.

'I'm very well thank you,' replied Max, under whelmed by his oldest friend's apparent lack of enthusiasm.

'You must be very happy,' continued Gerard.

'Yes I guess I am,' replied Max.

'I've only just come back from seeing Jordan,' continued Gerard, 'wonderful but the crew was so demanding. I have so much responsibility when I'm away, it's never a jolly,' Gerard exclaimed.

'I wouldn't know,' replied Max, 'in the twenty years I've known you I've never experienced a jolly while you travel the world. I can only assume.' Max felt annoyed that the subject of Gerard's work was once again the full remit of Gerard's conversation.

'Love when you're in media, your life is not your own,' moaned Gerard.

'About which Jordan are we talking?' Max asked.

'Love, Jordan the country. It's so beautiful and very spiritual,' Gerard responded. He was an undergraduate of ancient history and had received a first class honours at UCL and no longer believed in God so Max wondered to which type of spirit the reference was being made.

Max felt that either Gerard was playing with him or he really was jet lagged, so he let it slip. They had been friends for twenty years and had met at the Tunnel Club in Cardiff. It was the night when Paul O' Grady was a relatively unknown drag artist called Lilly Savage and Max and Gerard had laughed at the irreverence of the Myra Hindley impersonation. The pair had made love once. It was dreadful as you can't place two tops on a bottle of milk without it being difficult to open. They had decided to remain friends and after twenty years had both the closeness and the symbiosis that such friendships can develop.

Max thought a lot of Gerard but was aware of his limitations, he loved him, envied him and despaired of him with varying degrees of inconsistency. After twenty years Gerard would often drop into conversations that he had a first in history at London and that he would never have gone to university if he had not achieved a first. Max mused at his 2:2, a product of loathing Aberystwyth, whenever this was mentioned and even though Max now had a well respected doctorate Gerard would never cease to remind people of his now over twenty year old academic success. Gerard had been very kind about Max's doctorate and wanted to study for one himself, but like so much of his life, Gerard was now a fully fledged media slave and in spite of his moans, loved his work and the benefits it brought.

Max saw Gerard's academic aspirations a little differently since he met Cameron. For him Gerard was not an intellectual and had over compensated for this fact by acquiring reams and reams of knowledge. Gerard was well travelled and well spoken but at forty six had never had a relationship that had lasted longer than the cheese board at yet another swish London restaurant. Max envied him and pitied him for he knew that his friend who had declared his love for Max shortly before Robert had died, was a dear man but with so little emotional intelligence that he probably would never find someone strong enough and kind enough to make the effort to understand him and make him happy.

'So, can you come to the wedding,' Max asked, 'it's in August on the 7th, your parents are coming.'
'Oh I'd love to darling but I have a shoot in Florida. It's Key West again. I'll send my regards. Look love I'm running late. I'm very pleased for you but work calls. Gotta go. Love you loads.' Gerard rang off at that moment. Max sighed. For Max, that was duty to the 'family' out of the way and

as he reflected on the replies from his friends in London he realised his position. They had been friends when he was single. Robert was seen as the older gentleman who took care of Max but now Max was getting married to a beautiful young man. It was going to be official. Also Max was not as rich as he had been and Max felt sure that this was a factor in the text messages and lack of enthusiasm from his friend of twenty years. Cameron came downstairs looking unawake and beautiful.

'Morning darling,' Max said with a jaded sound in his voice.
'Morning darling,' replied Cameron. 'Are you OK? Give me a snog.'

The two kissed but there was a politeness in Max's affections that reflected his disappointment in the Londoners response to his news.

'Coffee?' Cameron asked.
'Oh yes that would be lovely,' Max replied.

The happy couple sat in the gallery room. This was an affectedly named room in Dr Max Hubbard-White's home but it reflected the fact that it was a narrow annex to the kitchen and dining room which led into the garden room and was furnished with contemporary Welsh art. Hence it had been declared a gallery.

'You seem low,' Cameron observed.

'Oh it's nothing,' Max replied, 'aren't you in work today?'

'Yes,' Cameron replied, 'but I'm four 'til close which could be 2.00 am. Now what's up?'

'Oh I just told the boys in London that we are having a civil ceremony,' said Max, his voice very subdued.

'Why can't you call it marriage?' asked Cameron.

'Because, I can't put it in italics like the Daily Mail and in any event, it's something legally new. It does not have a four thousand year religious history, it's British, twenty first century British and I like being accurate and I like the fact I'm doing it,' declared Max.

'Mmm so am I,' replied Cameron and the couple kissed as Benson, feeling decidedly out of the loop barked for attention.

'I felt today that I was communicating with people I love but they seemed from another planet,' retorted Max.

'Perhaps they don't like change,' comforted Cameron.

'Yes perhaps, but if one of my friends were embarking on something they felt was important I would at least make them feel that it was the best thing they had ever done. That's a friend's role. It's an honour,' bleated Max.

'There darling,' comforted Cameron, 'perhaps they haven't found someone they wanted to marry and they feel awkward. This is a new concept for people.'

Cameron was at his best when he saw Max in pain. He was so affectionate he could make Benson fall asleep in minutes when the beloved dog was at his most mischievous. He could have a similar effect on Max.

'They see you moving on, while their lives are the same. It doesn't matter how glamorous they are, you are happy and perhaps they can't deal with that after everything you've been through in the last four years,' Cameron offered.

'Yes my love, you have a point of course. I love you,' Max embraced his partner and felt a warmth and security that made him so happy.

'I love you Cameron,' he said, with an urgency in his tone.

'I adore you,' Cameron replied.

They made love in the gallery, amongst the Cannings and the Williams. Max thought it very risqué as the velux window had not been frosted and the drawing room of their muslim neighbours over looked the gallery.

Later that evening Max's mobile rang. It was Gerard.

'Hello love,' Gerard said.

'Hi Gerard,' Max answered in a low tone.

'I was not at my best this morning when we spoke,' Gerard continued. 'I just wanted to see if you are OK?' Gerard enquired.

'Yes of course,' Max replied. 'I'm very happy although I must say the boys seemed to be subdued about the announcement. Nobody has died.'

'I know,' continued Gerard, 'it's just a bit of a shock., I mean you've only known the man eighteen months,' offered Gerard.

'You have a commentary on eighteen month relationships Gerard?' asked Max.

'Darling I have a career,' replied Gerard.

'So does the President of the USA but he's married,' observed Max.

'Television is very invasive,' replied Gerard.

Max thought about the pending reality TV show about to descend on his well researched home.

'Yes, Cameron has been asked to be a contestant on 'Come Dine With Me,' replied Max.

'Well I hope that makes him happy,' replied Gerard in an enigmatic tone.

'I'm sure it will. So will I! I understand it receives great viewing figures for Channel Four,' stated Max.

'I'm sure it does,' replied Gerard, 'it must be so exciting for you.' Max felt patronised, gritted his teeth and continued.

'Oh I've decided to read a Susan Sontag book while filming is taking place,' replied Max, 'perhaps 'Illness and Its Metaphors.'

'I don't understand,' said Gerard,' I don't think you realise the importance of having a film crew at home.'

'No,' Max replied. 'I think that sentence went on far too long, you just don't think.'

'Darling, are you sure you're happy,' enquired Gerard.

'Oh yes, I'm very happy and thank you, I'm pleased that you are back at Key West, I'm sure you've been missed,' said Max, with an urgency in his voice. Max had paid for Gerard and him to take a first class trip to Key West a year after Robert died. Gerard loved the fuss but had actually tried to alter his ticket so that he could fly back later. Max had been furious over the lack of manners but on the phone that day it all seemed increasingly unimportant.

Gerard, seemingly oblivious to any concern Max may have had about the conversation asked, 'So have you heard from the boys?'

'Yes,' replied Max, 'Marcus and Charles both text me this morning. Charles was as always so gracious,' exclaimed Max.

'Yes and Marcus, you know he's just been promoted to Senior Producer for 'Smallkids TV'. He's such an angel,' observed Gerard.

'Lucifer?' offered Max.

'Darling, you must be exhausted with all the plans and the media coming?' asked Gerard.

'Yes,' replied Max, 'I'm wondering what drugs to get in for the occasion, have you any ideas, being in television?'

Laughter ensued from Gerard who then told Max that he had an urgent fax to the tourist board in Milan. Odd thought Max, he was sure that Gerard had been to Milan last year and had disliked the beauty of the place on the basis (and this was Max's interpretation), that nobody beautiful there had wanted to sleep with Gerard. Round two perhaps.

Max put the phone down. It was eight o' clock and Benson was sniffing around the back door. It was time for a walk. Max knew that he would never have children. He didn't mind this. He often observed the vanity that prefaced bad parenting and thought how unaware society was for loving children to the extent that parents forgot that they knew little and needed guidance. Here was his little Benson. In need, beautiful and barking for his dad's attention. Max picked up the lead, sending Benson into states of stretching and barking, the anticipation of the dog's trip to the park bringing a big smile to Max's face.

'Come on boy, let's take a walk, will you be page boy at daddies civil partnership?' Max asked the dog.

'Woof woof,' the dog replied and with that Benson licked Max's face. Max hugged him happily.

Chapter Six

It is a fact universally accepted that a man in possession of style is in need of a designer store.

Max and Cameron had chosen the Friday before the 'Come Dine With Me' experience to prepare for their wedding by buying their respective clothes and their wedding rings. Max knew that shopping on a Friday in Cardiff presented him with a somewhat problematic social dilemma as it marked the beginning of a complete change in demographics in the city centre. Those from Cardiff's hinterland prepared to descend upon the town for their own particular brand of festivities; the binge drinkers. For this reason they had chosen a ten o' clock start and the car was safely placed near their own shop of choice for the wedding clothes. This afforded them safety from the pending revellers and relief from the Thursday night trickles planning a long week end who would not rise before noon.

Flames was a large shop which possessed both an eclectic range of designer clothes and clientele. They entered the shop with Max choosing to wear a Prada jacket he had purchased there several months prior. He thought about his grandmother and her sense of smartness and manners but it also reminded the assistants that he was a regular, or at least had been. Max and Cameron were greeted by two eager eyed assistants who instantly measured their commission possibilities. Max hated this about shopping and had once had to be quite short with an ostensibly charming young man in Armani on New Bond Street who came into the changing cubicle when Max was half way through fitting a rather snug pair of jeans. 'Sir they really suit you, very Armani,' the young man had stated in earnest and with an east European accent. He had an air of omnipotent fashion expertise. Max had declined the purchase on the basis of the invasion reminding the assistant as he left the store that it was courteous in the UK not to enter a changing room without a written invitation and probably an affidavit in support.

Max and Cameron were polite yet uncommitted in their replies to the assistants and noticed a large black gentleman at the counter who had obviously done well for himself, purchasing over seven thousand pounds worth of what Max had identified as 'street', yet highly designed clothing, labels written boldly on the front of jackets and sweat shirts leaving the onlooker with no doubt as to their source. Max disapproved of such writing, which he instantly saw as a sign of insecurity in the wearer and the encouraging manipulation by the fashion house but Max had smiled at this and at the prolific shopper. The young man was overweight but had a certain sense of style that transcended size. He wore what Max had perceived was the obligatory 'hard man' gold jewellery and shades. He offered Max and Cameron a smile and looked very proud.

'Cameron,' Max asked his partner, 'that man has just spent over seven thousand pounds on clothes.'
'Yes darling,' replied Cameron, 'let's us off the hook a bit. We might be left alone for at least five minutes in the fall out.'

Max smiled at this. At least the assistants wouldn't be pressuring them after the young gentleman's purchases, he hoped. Max had often wondered about the 'street' or 'ghetto' mentality. He had enjoyed Fifty Cents whom he thought was quite a charming American. He believed completely that racism was a totally illogical concept and had often thought that the Race Relations Act was a complete misnomer. 'We are all the same race,' he had once stated to a less than inclusive dinner guest at Gerard's home. 'I believe the act should be called the Colour Prejudice Act, as it would identify the marginal difference between us and magnify the stupidity of the prejudice.' It had been met with a glare from some of the others and left Max concluding that intellectual abbreviation was endemic in the UK.

However Max did have a question that in spite of the young black man's apparent affable nature he felt would cause offence. The previous week Max had occasion to take an afternoon break and came across a programme entitled 'Cribs.' Thinking that it may be an expose on the quality of religious merchandise in the run-up to Christmas he had stopped the sky remote. It transpired that the programme examined the homes of many apparent celebrities, a lot of them being black Americans who had clearly become accomplished musicians. There were one or two people from the UK in the programme but Max had absolutely no idea who they were except the woman who declared herself Rod Stewart's daughter and Max thought that she had to be telling the truth and was worthy of inspection.

Max noted though that all the men who were 'wrap?' 'rapp' artists (he understood the concept but struggled with the lyrics) all lived in homes that had clearly been designed by Liberace. He had thought about his own elegant house in Llandaff and it's well researched furniture and colour schemes and he mused for a while that such ostentatious and definitely camp interiors of the 'cribs', which Max thought was a wonderful, if not perhaps disrespectful, reference to the bed holding the baby Jesus, were an expression of feminine appreciation from men who clearly went out of their way to represent masculine strength and toughness. He was confident that the irony may be lost on the young purchaser.

Max declined to pursue the matter with the young gentleman who had just noticed a pair of Gucci glasses which he added to his overall bill on the basis that he might think Max rude and thus game for physical exchanges. Max however was curious. He loved masculine things and even though his home was tastefully decorated, there was nothing there that suggested femininity or campness. Yet he had seen that for a straight man from a particular socio economic and racial background, extolling the experience of 'street' life and the music that represented it, resulted in his choice of interior design being feminine, very feminine. As gay as, Max had thought, smiling at his own circumspect prejudice which actually fell towards gay people rather than the optimistically entitled stars of Cribs.

Max and Cameron started to look. A D&G jacket exquisitely cut lay on the table priced at £1,200. 'That will cover the food, almost,' declared Max with an Amish sense of indignity in his voice, yet clearly he had fallen in love. 'Those two are making better clothes now they have separated,' he told Cameron as if they were regular dinner guests in their home.
'Yes,' Cameron replied, 'and I would look very good in it. Can we?' he asked.

'We cannot,' said Max sadly, hurt that his partner would have to make a compromise after years of Max's own spendthrift ways. Several years prior, when Robert had been alive, Max had purchased a Roberto Cavalli jacket in Harvey Nicholls. With ten per cent for opening an account with the store, the jacket had still cost over £2,500. Max had explained to a rather concerned Robert that it was a classic and therefore would last and that the charming assistant had offered him a free 'Orengina' while he waited for the item to be packed. The jacket was still good to run five years later and caused a stir when he wore it to dinner while on a ski trip in Canada. He felt torn inside but he had to be responsible for both of them and the wedding.

'Anyway,' said Max, 'it's grey and that such a drab colour for a wedding outfit.'
'True,' replied Cameron jadedly but conscious of their situation. They continued.

Eventually, Max found a very 'country gentleman' jacket with cream suede elbow patches that replicated the material just above the cuffs. Elegant he thought but festive and quirky. That'll be fine. I'm forty two, and thus well into gay middle age, educated and broke. Yes at £375.00 that'll do well I think. The purchase was made but alterations to the arms were required so the jacket was folded gently in tissue by the very well made up assistant with whom Max thought he had shared some previous physical intimacy but could not be sure so recoiled from the usual 'Alright mate,' which was an expression of gay inhibition and no doubt shame, that flowed easily from their straight counter parts, where in certain circles it constituted a genuine greeting.

Cameron then saw a beautiful blue jacket, very public school blazer with a white trim that came in small, ultra small and Maris from Frasier small. It almost prompted Max to ask the now attentive assistant, not resting on his laurels after the 'street' purchases, whether the Borrower's anorexic cousins had invaded town and opened a loyalty card. Cameron tried on the item and as it was on offer for £200.00 the purchase was made. They both then made a joint decision to go home and see if their extensive wardrobe provided them with matches for the purchases rather than run the risk of being declared indulgent and the assistants who were polite but understandably unimpressed by the £575.00 bill, carefully wrapped (yes Max thought, its 'rapp') the blue jacket in tissue paper and bagged it. Max paid.

'Rings next!' declared Max with an element of 'we're doing well and that last experience was an achievement' in his voice. Max belied the rather prescriptive concept that gay men liked shopping. He had shopped a lot in his time but he couldn't stand let alone understand those people whom appeared to genuflex at window displays. It was heretical and almost as bad at that other shopping hazard, the dawdlers. He tolerated it on the roads as he knew that a lot of older people had at least four days in which to arrive at any of their destinations but in the shopping centres it was a hazard worthy of a segregation policy which he felt should now be a matter for the Government. He had tried shopping with his solicitor friend Eliza once for shoes which had ended in him retreating home early and consuming quite quickly, half a bottle of Oban scotch.

The dawdlers were obviously still in bed contemplating dreams and visions of ambling aimlessly along the High Street with no sense of purpose but just to gaze and digest their environment blissfully unaware of how tragic they were. Max and Cameron made good speed, Max's mind always beset with the parking costs.

Max was a focused shopper. Research the shops, find people with whom you could hold a conversation and execute. Short, effective and efficient. For this reason, the purchasing of the rings had been a straight forward exercise. Max was of an age where only one shop in

Cardiff would be appropriate for civil partnership bands and that was Crouches. As a child he had often come to Cardiff with his mother to tax cars that were newly purchased from his father's car sales business. The tax office had been positioned on the second floor of a grand classical looking building half way along St Mary's Street. It was now a gentleman's outfitters. Opposite had been Crouches, the diamonds, the watches, the clocks, all sparkling, all a world away from Max's five pounds per week pocket money which even then had been considered generous. Max headed for the store.

To Max's dismay, the store was now a branch of the eatery known as McDonalds. Max paused for a moment. Had it been so long since he had undertaken a shopping trip to town. He had been through some financial hardship during the last year and was down to only three houses but surely something as iconic as Crouches could not have fallen foul to any recession. He felt a pit grow in his stomach as the expectations of his youth, to purchase his wedding ring from Crouches, seemed taken. The thought of purchasing online or worse still a high street store became overwhelming for Max and he turned to Cameron.

'Cameron, I think we should come back to town another day, I can't believe that Crouches is no more,' he said with deep reflection in his voice. 'I wanted you to have a ring from Crouches because when I was a child I knew it was the best jewellers and I wanted you to know that you deserved the best I knew.' Max was actually wiping away tears at this point.

'Darling,' soothed Cameron, 'there is a Crouches in the shopping mall.'

'Oh no,' replied Max, 'I'm sure there isn't.'

'Yes there is, it's one of the corner shops in St David's 2,' replied Cameron.

'Darling, I'm sure Crouches wouldn't do such a thing as shopping malls, it's a Cardiff institution. Are you sure it's not someone else?' Max asked now a little drier in his eyes but still feeling thwarted.

'Let's go and have a look, I'm sure it's there,' responded Cameron.

When Max entered one of the side doors at the new St. David's 2, which had not been universally accepted in the city as constituting progress, the warmth of the lights and the professional displays made Max feel that Cardiff had entered a new level of commercialism which both emancipated it in the global market of retail and relegated it in the ever marginalised world of spirituality. Max had seen the centre being built from the sitting room of a friend whose apartment overlooked the city centre. The space had been amazing when all the previous buildings had been demolished and Max had thought how wonderful it would be to have an enormous fountain and formal park in the area with just a few three storey shops around the outside, something along the lines of the Grand Place in Brussels. Instead Cardiff had been provided with a much more utilitarian mecca for the retailers.

'Darling I'm not convinced Crouches would be found here, look there's a Pizza Hut,' exclaimed Max in a very Dame Maggie Smith tone.
'Look!' said Cameron with an excitement in his voice which made Max both beam and bust to his very core, 'see, it's on the corner.'

Max looked. For a moment, he couldn't believe that one of the city's flag ship shops had been transported, probably courtesy of the local Dr Who team, to the St David's 2 shopping mall, but there it was. Max stopped and then walked with slight reservation toward the window. He

Timothy Brown

held Cameron's hand and was completely oblivious to the potential for ambivalence it may cause.

'There darling,' exclaimed Max. 'It's white gold, middle depth and affordable. It's £700.00 for the two.' Max sighed and waited for a moment as he realised that not only was this old jewellery store still operating, albeit in reduced circumstances in his opinion, but he could actually go in and purchase the rings for him and Cameron. Max felt a tear in his eye which he passed off as a consequence of the perfume department at Debenhams secreting it's usual anti ozone fumes.

Max and Cameron gingerly entered the shop. It was very slick but Max felt that this new corporate motif detracted from the seventies icon that lit up the main street. Crouches, Marments, Howells, the Cardiff of Max's youth. As he shopped, he thought that these parents of retail had been modified or even forgotten. No more Gold Card room at Howells. Democracy can be so disruptive. No Marments, well it was bridal but Max was feeling the occasion as a conservative man, and here was Crouches, still wonderful, but placed amongst the corporate Atillas who had no sense of history Max was sure. Shopping was no longer an occasion but now merely a fraught adventure which moulded the public's spending rather than deferred to it. Nevertheless as a child of the seventies, here he was in Crouches, amongst the memories of his aspiring middle class childhood. He felt good. He breathed out.

The shop assistant was called Dorothy. A rather prescriptive omen, thought Max but he smiled at her and afforded her the courtesies which he felt confident would be perceived as odd by the, 'I'm the customer do as I want, brigade.' She spoke, 'So you are looking for wedding bands?' her enquiry seemed benign.
'Yes,' replied Max.
'So who's getting married?' she asked.
'We are,' replied Max, 'to each other.'

Dorothy blushed a little. Max wondered if in the capital of Wales they had been the first gay couple to commit legally to each other. He and Cameron had once taken five minutes to make a very embarrassed hotel receptionist in Preston realise a double room was fine. Max deflected the obvious embarrassment. 'That's a beautiful ring you're wearing,' he said.
'Oh thank you,' replied Dorothy, 'the diamonds are South African.'

'Like mine,' Max offered.

'Excuse me?' Dorothy asked.

'Oh Cameron is South African by birth and he's my diamond,' offered Max in the spirit of the occasion.

'Oh, well we have incorrectly priced the rings as the price of gold has increased,' stated Dorothy, and she immediately stood up and left the shop floor.

'I'll be back in a minute,' she said.

Max looked at Cameron. 'Have we created an incident here? Shall we now be hell fire and brim stoned by the evangelical jewellery organisation, purveyors of rings to the Pope and Billy Graham?' he asked.

'She looked very unsettled,' replied Cameron, 'perhaps she can't share in the joy or identify with us,' he continued

'Perhaps we should have written to Paul O Grady and asked him for some costume diamante cast offs,' joked Max.

'Too impractical,' replied Cameron, who Max felt was feeling guarded at this point.

Dorothy returned. The couple sat uneasily.

'I'm really sorry but the rings have been incorrectly priced and I had to check that it was alright for me to sell them to you at the price in the window,' she offered with sincere empathy in her voice.

Max's mind went straight into law lecturer mode. She was in an awkward position. Legally, when items are for sale in a shop window, they are not 'on offer' but are 'on invitation to treat'. He had often made his students laugh by reflecting on all those special offers in Tesco and M and S that were misnamed and should have read, 'on special invitation to treat.' This meant that the shop had no legal obligation to sell the goods at the misprice even when the goods were priced at a lower amount, something which your average not to mention uninformed shopper, would contest, even to the point of violence. It was a criminal offence to misprice goods yes, but there was no contractual obligation. Circumspect as ever, Max interjected.

'Oh well,' he said, 'I quite understand your position, what is the actual price?'

Dorothy's eyes seemed to mist for a moment.

'You know with the constant fluctuation in gold prices, it's been so difficult to keep the gold and silver accurately priced in the shop.' Dorothy was clearly distressed.

'Dorothy,' began Max, 'I don't want to have to sell my BMW, but I'm sure that we can accommodate a small increase in the price.' Max was feeling paternalistic at this point, the woman was clearly feeling the pain of this revelation in retail manners.

'No,' replied Dorothy, 'I've spoken with the manager and we are happy to offer you the rings at the stated price and because we have caused you confusion I was determined to get you a 10% discount.'

If it wasn't for Max's conservative disposition he would have kissed Dorothy, not just for her discount which was a welcomed addition to the ceremony's drinks fund but because it also showed her complete lack of prejudice in her role as facilitator for the 'big day'. This lady had brought Max's own insecurities about prejudice to the edge and then in one moment of ten per centing had made him feel like a man who was going to be married and here was a random stranger who, while wanting a sale, had gone out of her way for them. In doing that she had shown a sensitivity and respect that completely fulfilled and even exceeded Max's expectations of the old store. He had made the right choice. He felt decades of manners and service honed in on this very moment. He felt respected and he felt good. Dorothy packed the rings in ceremonial fashion and wished Cameron and Max all the very best for the future. The purchase was made and Cameron and Max would be wearing Flames jackets and Crouches rings at their civil ceremony. The past and the present were fused, now to the future.

On their way back to the car, Max turned to Cameron.

'A very productive day Mr Stewart,' he said.
'I totally agree,' Cameron replied.
'I feel very grown up,' said Max.
'You are,' replied Cameron.

As they got into the car Max thought about Cameron's last comment. Yes, he thought, I might be of an age where being a grown up is assumed, but today the child in him needed to feel good as well. It was because he was growing up and entering a brand new stage in his life. He was glad that the experiences and joys of his youth had moulded his thoughts as a man. Dorothy had made him and Cameron feel like any excited couple about to commit and Max reflected that in a world of prejudice he and Cameron could be treated like any other couple. He turned on Classic FM and Mendelsohn's 'Wedding'

music from Shakespeare's A Midsummer Night's Dream'
was being aired.

'See,' said Max to Cameron, 'the fairies approve I think.'
The couple drove home happy and more at ease that their
civil ceremony was now in that eve stage.

Max parked his BMW on Palace Rd which ran adjacent
to their home. With bags shared equally between them
they proceeded to take the short journey to their home.
As they passed their neighbours house, a mini van of
weekenders passed by on the other side heading into
town.

'Oiy faggot,' one shouted and then the mini van shook
as the other occupants, equally vitriolic shouted similar
obscenities at them. Max looked at the mini van and
made out that it came from Bridgend. He looked around
at the cars queuing and the looks people were giving the
men in the mini van. Value neutral, Max later thought
as he relayed their experience to a very nice police officer
called Sam. Max got into his house and felt shaken. In
broad day light after such a wonderful outing to town,
this had happened. Cameron was thicker skinned than

Max and shrugged the incident off with an appeal to Max sense of social expectation.

'Look darling, there we were, happy carrying designer bags and they just thought lets make them miserable. Don't let them, they looked drunk.'

'And from Bridgend,' interjected Max, 'so clearly troubled.' Cameron laughed, but Max's efforts to make light of it belied his feelings towards the judgemental attitude of some of his fellow countryman. 'Land of My Fathers,' he thought, 'they can keep it.'

A few days later Max felt more measured about the incident. Their house was now placed on a police priority list because the young men in the van had seen them entering their home. The CCTV was useless but the police words of assurance seemed sincere at least. Max looked over at Cameron, 'I thought about the woman in the shop, polite, very accomplished in her job, tasteful and wishing us every happiness. I focused on the positive for once and now I feel better. I can't wait to commit to you at my own City Hall.'

Chapter Seven

'What about bite size fish and chips?' Max enquired with Cameron whom Max had concluded was far the superior partner in terms of culinary affairs, something now affirmed by the seemingly omnipotent coming of the validating media.

'What for?' asked Cameron.
'The reception,' replied Max, 'its traditional Saturday food, with a hint of cultivated ordinariness that is unpretentious. It's good for the vegetarians who eat fish and everyone will be comfortable with it.'

The look of relief on Cameron's face as he realised this was not one of Max's well intentioned but scholastically illiterate contributions to his pending media experience was obvious and yet a little grilling.

'I thought you could do the out size variety for the show,' Max continued mockingly.

Cameron's eyes sharpened for a moment. The bunnies were still going to boil whether Max liked it or not.

'Well I suppose the Saturday night theme is acceptable,' said Cameron, 'and our families will be grateful for the gesture.'

Max and Cameron came from different backgrounds in many ways. Cameron was brought up in South Africa by parents who loved to travel, while Max was a true Brit, with a slightly insular perspective. He could not understand why Europeans left Europe unless it was for work or to help the poor and America and Canada of course were British territories which had grown up, so that was acceptable and they spoke English, with varying degrees of success. On one thing however they were united, Saturday nights meant take out. As a child Max had loved the feeling of standing between his two large grandparents as cod and hake were ordered and the memory of the anticipation of the wrapped food on the journey home made the fish and chip supper integral to his weekly, or sometimes fortnightly, diet.

'Bite size fish and chips it is then,' declared Max.

'They are called *goujons,*' stated Cameron with the authority of one who had made the position of meeting and events manager at a local four star hotel.

'I have read Hemmingway my dear and I'm sure that means that we would be providing a very different sort of reception,' said Max with a grin on his face.

Cameron loved Max but there were times when Max felt that his beloved partner would one day seek out a carer's allowance because of Max's tangential humour.

'We need vegetarian and vegan and wheaten free,' declared Cameron.

'Are we inviting feminist lesbians?' enquired Max.

'Yes, but they have the courtesy of eating anything,' Cameron replied with a giggle in his voice.

'Yes said Max, 'we have progressive friends don't we.'

'It's my mother,' stated Cameron, 'she has to be wheat free.'

'Ill cancel the hay bails then,' Max offered, this time resulting in a waspish look from Cameron.

Max was feeling a little pressured as the big day was less than seven weeks away and the media were coming first. The 'Come Dine With Me' experience Max had only seen once when he got confused after switching on the television and thought that Edwina Curry and Christopher Biggins were in a documentary looking at Conservative censorship of Pantomime.

'What about meat?' Max asked.

'Yes,' replied Cameron.

'I agree,' replied Max. With that he opened the door leading to the end of the garden room where a very excited Benson was about to give his contribution to the preparations by lifting his leg dangerously close to a beautiful chaise which Max had purchased in Howells. The poor dog must have sensed the endless revisions of the ceremony and was clearly feeling rejected.

'Out for pee pees please,' prompted Max with an edge in his voice. Benson dutifully responded. Max followed him.

The garden room was south facing and the day had evolved from an overcast beginning into a glorious sunny July day. Max's garden was small for the size of the house, a product of Victorian over building. Builders never change he thought; profit before people. The garden had been laid in a very practical way with a car port at the end, essential to hide the convertible from potential, albeit tasteful, car thieves. There was a small raised border in the middle which housed some beautiful standard roses and a miniature weeping willow. Nearer the house was a paved area which held an oval table seating ten. Max and Robert had purchased it five years prior at the Royal Horticultural Show in Cardiff. The young man had been a persuasive factor in the purchase and Max smiled. Yes he had been a spend thrift but what taste. There was a voice.

'Hi Max,' it was Michaela, 'how are all the plans going?'

'For what exactly?' enquired Max.

'The wedding,' replied Michaela.

'Oh I have booked the weather,' replied Max flippantly. Michaela laughed.

'I've bought a new hat,' Michaela announced.

'Wow a hat!' exclaimed Max, 'that's serious, I hadn't contemplated hat wearing.'

'It's a wedding,' Michaela replied.

'Well let's keep it as a civil partnership,' Max said, with a speech welling within him, 'I know it gives us the same rights as a married couple, but marriage has a particular tradition which involves a man and a woman and often a priest. Our legal commitment is only six years old and very twenty first century Britain and we wouldn't want to encroach.'

'Well Stefan and I see it as a marriage,' Michaela said unrepentant.

'That's because you are a good catholic woman,' offered Max, smiling at the idea of a papal blessing at the occasion.

'Stefan was down to work that week end but he has changed shifts so that he can attend. Is it alright for the children to come? Michaela asked.

This was something for which Max had not budgeted. There were two schools of thought about children at weddings. One was that they were an integral part of the family setting and often provided the parents with an opportunity to over dress them in a Victorian manner making the children look like extras in Narnia. The other was that children mitigated the fun as they were a responsibility and messed up the flowers. Max understood the ideal of the former but was a close advocate of the latter, and of course it was a 'gay wedding.' He thought quickly.

'Well that would be lovely. It seems a shame not to have them here and I'm sure they will be the centre of attention,' he offered generously. They were beautiful children and well parented. This proved to be a wise decision.

'We've booked a baby sitter for them as well,' Michaela offered as a mitigation to any shock she perceived Max might have had about the idea.

'That's expedient,' replied Max clearly feeling that there was at least a plan B to counter any short comings in his evaluation of their presence at the event.

'Now is there anything you need?' enquired Michaela. About an extra five grand thought Max but he politely said, 'No, it's all going to plan thanks.' He knew the offer was sincere but actually, he and Cameron had successfully accomplished the major aspects of the preparations, the caterer was booked, the clothing purchased and the rings were being modified to fit their slender than average fingers.

Max went into the kitchen, poured himself a large scotch (well it was after seven in India he thought), and went back outside to enjoy the sun and a very relaxed Benson. As he took the first taste, Max felt the warmth of the liquid slip down his throat which made his shoulders shiver and then fall into a more comfortable position. The garden roses were few in number as Max's gardening skills stopped at dead heading and watering. Both could be undertaken with a G&T so it was sociable gardening. He had declared himself an expert in it to his friends.

Max heard Cameron in the background prepare for a rehearsal dinner for his media engagement and his teeth began to grind. His outward appearance was calm and in the tranquil surroundings of his middle class, comfortable existence, the safety, the warmth, he looked up at his home and his mind wandered. It was nearly two years since he had almost met with his own end here in this very house. He began to relive the events that had passed between him and a young man called Jimmy.

Jimmy had been introduced to Max just over two years prior by his friend Eliza. Max had been asked to give Jimmy advice on a potential winding-up situation in a building company Jimmy ran and Eliza, much to Max's constant dismay, had informed Jimmy that Max was gay. Jimmy was lodging with Eliza while yet another flat (he had lived in many it later transpired) was being prepared and had walked into the sitting room at Eliza's water side home topless, but just putting on a tee shirt. It was not the first time a 'straight' guy had tried to win influence with Max by being sexually overt and Max at first pitied Jimmy's efforts. He was not an unattractive man, in fact he had that air of cockiness that for most builders was an integral part of their perceived charm. His accent was Sussex but not Hove or Worthing but somewhere far less fashionable.

Max had introduced himself and spent a few hours with Jimmy looking at alternatives to the pending liquidation such as administration or an IVA. Jimmy seemed more interested in finding a way to set up another company and bank account and writing off his responsibilities. Max was aware that 'phoenix syndrome' while unlawful was practised by many, particularly in the building trade as the concept was very difficult to police. Max had even appeared on a BBC consumer affairs programme discussing the issue. He was not impressed by Jimmy's attitude but nor was he impressed about the law in this area.

Two days after they met Max received a telephone call from Jimmy who had needed some further advice from Max and asked if Max would view some papers for him. As it was a Friday and Max had no plans he had wanted to advise Jimmy on the more acceptable not to mention legal alternatives to Jimmy's plans, so he agreed to meet him at Eliza's. When Max arrived, Jimmy was looking very wide eyed and pleased to see Max.

'Where's Eliza?' asked Max.
'Mums gone to London,' replied Jimmy.

Max disliked this about Jimmy. He had taken to calling Eliza 'Mum,' as she had clearly taken him in and because she was over twenty years older than he. It was clearly the closest concept to admiration with which Jimmy could provide her. Max thought it patronising and felt that Eliza's feelings were far more ambiguous towards the man.

Max then heard water coming from upstairs. Jimmy had run a bath in Eliza's room. The bath was a circular tub of six feet in diameter and had been lifted onto a lorry and delivered to Eliza's home stopping the traffic for an hour in the Bay. It was lit up from the sides and Max had once sat in it admiring the view across the Bay to Cardiff's city centre. It was possible to denote some hotels and the Millenium Stadium from that bath and Max felt sure this would be a selling point for Eliza who had filled the bathroom and the rest of the house with discerning modern art and other objet d'art. The house and the bedroom/bathroom were modern and not completely to Max's taste but Eliza was a law unto herself and like Max was meticulous in her research when it came to designing a home. Max liked her, although often she would leave him shaking his head in disbelief at some of her ideas. She was a gay man in a woman's body and thus sought honorary membership to the lavender club. Max suspected that Jimmy would be one such idea of hers that would leave him feeling depressed.

Jimmy's quarters were on the ground floor of this three storey bay side home. Max had thought it very presumptuous that Jimmy would run a bath in Eliza's own quarters but Max believed that Jimmy had authority for this otherwise he would not have been so confident in front of Max. Max and Eliza went back twenty years and were confirmed allies.

Max felt uneasy as Jimmy opened a bottle of champagne. He also had another bottle next to it. It was plastic and empty with a hole in the side.

'What's that?' asked Max.

'It's for purifying cocaine,' answered Jimmy with a presumptuous boldness that made Max feel uneasy yet excited.

'Why would you want that?' Max asked naively,

'To ensure that there are no impurities,' replied Jimmy.

The next thing Max knew, the bottle was being filled to with two inches of water and a foil cap was being placed on top. Jimmy placed a cigarette lighter on top of the foil.

'This is the real stuff,' he declared, pleased with his dexterity.

'What is it?' Max asked curiously.

'Pure cocaine,' replied Jimmy as he took off his shirt, 'try some.'

Max feeling both reserved and still excited, inhaled some of the smoke formulating in the plastic bottle. He had many media friends and had taken one or two lines in the past, but he was a man of habit and he hated the fact that the substance kept him up too late and made Max far too animated.

'Breath in deeply,' encouraged Jimmy, 'otherwise it will be a waste.'

Max breathed deeply. As a smoker he felt a natural instinct to keep the fumes in his mouth for as long as possible and practised a gulping which took in the smoke incrementally. As he withdrew from the task set, he felt giddy and opened up. Jimmy smiled. 'It's better pure,' he explained.

'Gosh that's good, I feel so well,' offered Max.
'You need to relax with it,' exclaimed Jimmy, 'ready to bathe?'

The bottle and the men decamped upstairs where the lighting in Eliza's bathroom had been dimmed. The two men undressed and got into the warm water. The plastic bottle had been brought up and was lying on the side next to the champagne. It all appeared intoxicating and exciting.

The two felt the warmth of the bubbling water around them as Jimmy lit another bottle top and offered it to Max, 'You gotta keep things up,' he stated and Max, feeling so enclosed and warm followed Jimmy's instructions and was beginning to feel amazing; so calm, so confident, so alive and in control. He noticed Jimmy's naked body. He was a small man about five seven, but toned and with the most beautiful backside. Max felt sexual. Jimmy noticed Max looking and lent across him in the steroidal bath with a grin on his face.

'Yea that'ta boy,' said Jimmy, 'let's have some fun.'

The two men talked, caressed and fondled for the next eight hours until at five in the morning, Max declared that he had to go. Feeling defensive yet so sexual he called a taxi leaving his BMW without care and headed for home. That had been the start of his Crack habit. It was June and he had no idea of the damage that had been reeked upon his mind that night. He had stopped for cigarettes on the way home, his nose red at the tip and his eyes so dilated.

The next five months were hell for Max. The intoxication and the expectation of sex led to a frequent grinding of teeth, sleepless nights and long afternoons asleep. Jimmy would call a lot but they only had sex on two further occasions after that leaving Jimmy to declare that Max was being manipulative. The crack had come with great infrequency and as Max craved more and more, Jimmy would be less and less available.

Jimmy's main argument for avoiding sex was that he had a daughter and that he owed it to her not to have sex with men. The fact that Jimmy used his sexuality to cultivate clients did not mitigate Max's sense of guilt that he was hooked to crack cocaine. After five months, Max knew that he had a problem and sort help. The first call was made to Frank, which had been advertised on the BBC as a drugs helpline. All Max got from a very sensorial man was that cocaine was illegal and that the maximum penalty was five years imprisonment. That was of no help, Max needed a formula, a person to assist him getting off the drug. His next call was to an organisation that believed that the answer to Max's compulsion was to become a Roman Catholic. What Max thought, would changing his beliefs on trans-substantiation and the infallibility of the Pope help with his desperation. Jimmy was still in touch and Max increasingly felt remote, ashamed and desperate.

The last night Jimmy and Max met, it had started the usual way. Max had bought two bottles of scotch and Jimmy had brought the cocaine. Max had paid him £300 for the festivities and Jimmy gladly accepted the money. At three in the morning and after more fumblings, Jimmy went for more drugs. Max anticipated at home. Drunk and pacing the kitchen, Jimmy arrived ashen faced. He had been 'done over' by two youths whom Jimmy explained were symptomatic of the crack dealing culture. He immediately demanded £100 from Max.

'Why?' asked Max naively, 'I've already paid you.'
'I've been done,' replied Jimmy, 'and I owe.'
'I'm sorry said Max but I can't get anything tonight but I can get something in the morning.'

With that Jimmy exploded into a rage and Max, usually so phlegmatic in his attitude to people barked back, 'Get out of my home, you are boring me, you are so predictable, I'm not going to be a victim and I'm not going to be your victim, get the hell out of my house.'

Jimmy immediately dialled his phone while Max headed for his. Within five minutes of continued shouting a figure appeared outside the front door. It was a man, tall and young with black hair. He looked Italian or maybe Greek. Jimmy looked darkly at Max and the door was opened. There stood the man about twenty five. Max noticed a gun in the man's hand.

'A non payer?' he asked Jimmy.
'Yes,' Jimmy replied.

The gun was held against Max until he agreed to get the money. The cash point was in the village and it was now four in the morning. Max protested that he owed nothing but to no avail. He was frog marched up to the cash point and he withdrew the money. Jimmy demanded some clothes that were in Max's house. They walked back down the road to Max's home. Max felt sick and yet relieved that if he was going to be killed his shame would be at an end.

As Jimmy picked up his clothes, the young man raised the gun but Jimmy told him to leave Max alone and went out of the house shouting homophobic ranting at Max. Max closed the door and slipped to the floor. He must have staid there for an hour before climbing slowly to his knees. He staggered upstairs to his bed. He collapsed.

It was early Sunday morning before Max came around. He was cold and hungry. He reached for the phone to call the police but then thought of the consequences. *They* knew where he lived. He turned over and tried to sleep again but by three o clock he was so hungry that he went downstairs. He ate. He thought. This is the lowest point and I can't get up from it. It's got to end, but there are plans first. The strength and discipline that were so important to the continuation of Max's life could not be forgotten even when he was planning his own demise.

The following day was Monday and Max had woken with a sense of relief. He was happy, relaxed and knew what he had to do. He had some important classes to teach and he successfully managed that making his students laugh about Marquis of Bute's case and it's insight into directors' duties. He finished work, came home and wrote his will. He disinherited his sister and gave his estate to charity. He visited Stefan and Michaela as he needed independent signatories. Michaela looked at him oddly, 'Are you OK Max?' she asked.
'Yes I'm good thanks,' Max replied, 'just thought its time I sorted things out. I haven't altered my will since Robert died.' As he left Michaela gave him a big hug. 'You know we are always here if you want to talk,' she offered and Max's eyes brimmed with tears.

He returned home, did some cleaning, watered the plants, then went upstairs into his gym which had been converted from a fifth bedroom. A chair had been placed in front of the TV. Max waited. At midnight he started to take anti depressants. Two at first, then a sip of scotch, two more, then another sip. It was blended. Max had mused that one of his concerns was that he would be found with an empty bottle of blended scotch next to him. He smiled, the relief was gaining. Another two and a sip. This went on for three hours until he had taken over forty anti depressants and the bottle was nearly empty. He text a few friends, 'Thank you for everything, I love you, I just can't love me anymore, I'm sorry.' He had chosen this later hour as he knew everyone would be in bed. He closed his eyes.

Max then heard the phone ring. It was nearly four and he picked it up. It was Caroline, one of his closest friends whom he had texted.

'Where are you?' she asked, 'I'm at your front door with the police.'

Max ambled down the stairs. He was barely ten stone and was wearing running leggings and a black tee shirt. He looked emaciated. Caroline and the policemen faced Max with a look of horror on their face as Max unburdened himself of the previous forty eight hours. The four got into the police car as Max, pulling on a chunky old jacket, looked around. His shame was complete but he knew what he had done and he hoped that he would not be back at his home later. He took one last look at his well researched abode and the car sped to the hospital.

Two hours of sensitive talking and tests showed that Max's fitness levels and lack of weight had meant that the drugs had not taken a strong effect. The blood test showed that Max's life was not threatened but the hospital wanted to keep Max in for observations. Max protested but stayed a night at the drugs unit where to his surprise a smoking room was provided. Every cloud, thought Max to himself. The following day, text messages had poured in from his friends and he realised that people cared enough for him to believe that it was worth caring about himself. He had gone back to his home, nervous but determined, depressed still but this time with a source of strength inside him that had been the same strength that had reacted to Jimmy, eventually. He looked at his sitting room; the art, the furniture, the tableau, all so beautiful and yet since Robert's death, all so meaningless.

The home was now a house and Max realised that this was the source of his downfall. He wept.

That had been nearly two years ago. As Cameron called him from the kitchen, he wiped his eyes as the sun seemed to ease him back to his home with a gentle warm pat on the back. Max felt lucky. The house was a home again. Cameron had made it so. He was not depressed any longer but he was angst about the upcoming weeks. He smiled at Cameron who knew instantly where Max was. They embraced, kissed and held each other very tightly.

Chapter Eight

The book of Genesis had made it quite clear. The earth was formed by God in seven days. It was unclear how long each day was but it completely failed to disclose the fact that God had wanted to take a little longer. Ah, Max had thought, that explains Belgium. The reason for God's hurry, Max later thought, was that he was on a schedule and once Max had seen the schedule for the pending reality TV experience he realised that it was not exclusive to the Almighty; on time, with a few mishaps. Revisions would be required.

The objective of the 'Come Dine With Me', competition as Max had been told by the director, an ebullient lady called Sarah, was that five contestants would invite random strangers to their individual homes through a working week period and cook dinner. Random strangers and dinner sounded very much like Max's social life during the eighties but on relaying this to Cameron he was relieved to discover that sex was not an expectation after pudding. However giving points for effort was. Some things never change, thought Max.

Cameron had been preparing with the bunnies and pheasant and was intent on making something called a pativier. Recoiling from any further input to the menu Max had sat in awe as Cameron busied himself in the kitchen. The preparation was endless and Cameron was to be the finale on the Friday night. Max received a text. It was from his friend Howard. Max had texted him when Cameron received the news about the filming and Howard was now texting to declare that he also had been a chosen one.

'They've been badgering me for weeks,' Howard moaned on his confirming telephone call ten minutes later, 'so I thought well why not. It's for the kids'
'But you don't have any kids!' questioned Max.
'Caroline's four,' replied Howard.
Max always rolled his eyes at this. Howard was gay and yet had this over arching desire to appear straight to fulfil, Max assumed, the expectations of his father who had invested heavily in Howard's public school education.

Max was a little perplexed at this particular call. He knew Howard had experience of reality TV taking the part of a school master in one of those 'What was it like to live in the past' programmes. Read a book, Max had thought, but said nothing. He called into the kitchen where apparently Cameron was mid flow with an Italian ice cream mix.

'Howard is another one of the contestants next week darling,' said Max anticipating a reply. Nothing came. 'Did you hear me?' Max asked.

Cameron appeared at the arch way between the kitchen and the sitting room. Face solid, eyes cold. If ever there had been a gay pin up for conscription he would have been it.

'So he waits to tell us now!' exclaimed Cameron.
'Yes, he said that the TV company has been badgering him for weeks,' replied Max.
'Well aren't we all just privileged to be accepting his company into our home' replied Cameron and he turned almost allowing the white mix to imprint onto the London Stone paint but Farrow and Ball escaped as Max

heard the hand whisk produce an electric intensity in the kitchen.

Howard and Cameron were not close. This was partly to do with the fact that they rarely saw each other but also Howard had extended an invitation to Max, after Robert's death, to form a much closer alliance. Cameron was unconvinced that Howard's motives towards Max had changed but he had always been pleasant to him, always made an effort. After twenty minutes, which Max thought was a reasonable time for the ice cream to settle, he went into the kitchen where Cameron was smoking a cigarette.

'Hey,' said Max, 'in the fine tradition of Jennifer Patterson I see, and you're slim.' Cameron looked at Max with an effort to make a kind response in his eyes but failing.
'Darling, do you mind next week?' asked Cameron.
'No of course not, why would I?' countered Max and knelt at Cameron's side.
'I'll be out every night,' said Cameron.
'Well you're twenty eight darling, you should have a social life,' said Max with a smile.
'You sure you'll be alright?' asked Cameron.

'I'll be fine. Now you go and win the, what's the prize money?' asked Max.

'One thousand pounds,' said Cameron., 'I can pay off my overdraft.'

'Or buy your shortly-to-be civil partner a wonderful wedding gift,' Max said and laughed.

'Why would Howard let us know so late? The invitations were made weeks ago,' asked Cameron.

'Perhaps he wanted to make an entrance. Note his comments, 'They've been badgering me for weeks,' as if he was some seasoned Hollywood actor who had semi retired because he had found God.' Cameron smiled at this. His eyes were a little blood shot as he had been practising his recipes for the big night and working all day.

Monday came around very quickly and during the day there was a feeling that the ghost of Christmas past was about to descend on Max's home. Cameron took an hour to get ready for the first evening which was themed as a beach party.

'In north Cardiff?' asked Max. 'How optimistic.' Cameron had chosen long trousers, based on the idea that for every Benidorm in the world there is a Palm Springs. He looked beautiful and left the house in a taxi booked by the show at seven pm.

'Best of luck,' Max offered as Cameron kissed Benson goodbye.

'Thank you darling,' replied Cameron, 'don't wait up.'

Max sat down and opened a bottle of scotch around eight and he and Benson settled in to watch 'It's a Beautiful Life.' Benson seemed to follow the sub titles very well, looking occasionally up at Max with a genuine look of sympathy on his face. He almost had an accident when the boy and his mother were united at the end.

It was a quarter to four in the morning when Max felt a light kiss on his fore head. The television had long gone onto stand by and as Max opened his eyes, Benson made a strategic foot step that made Max wake with acceleration.

'Hi Darling,' Cameron said, 'let's go to bed.'

'How did it go?' asked Max.

'Really well but I'm tired now, can we sleep?' Cameron's eyes were now very blood shot and Max immediately felt that one thousand pounds could not be worth all this; still four days to go and Cameron would be preparing on the Friday. Max was concerned but knew that if he challenged Cameron he would get his grandmother's reply, 'I'm not made of sugar.'

The next three nights were replications. Cameron would leave at seven and arrive home around three thirty bleary eyed and exhausted. The information gleaned by the Friday was that one contestant had received breast enhancements. 'For the chicken?' Max had asked Cameron. Another contestant lived with many teddy bears and had no children and Howard. Max and Cameron were all too well aware of the psychoses underpinning him. He had been the Tuesday and Max thought had produced a much more competitive feast of traditional lamb.

Howard and Max went back twenty years. They had attempted sex on two occasions but at neither point had there been a satisfactory conclusion. Max had moved during the incidents, a courtesy he afforded to all of his lovers, whereas Howard had not and this, Max thought, lacked manners. There was also the victim status which Max felt a lot of gay men gravitated towards on the basis that at some point someone had been less than kind to them because of their sexuality. Max had also been a victim of this in his time and was still sensitive to name calling or sometimes worse, being patronised, but over the years, he had focused on the positive when this happened and realised that for everyone that went out of their way to be unkind, there were people out there who just didn't care and thus remained passive in their attitudes toward gay people, not because they didn't want happiness for all but because they were probably struggling to obtain happiness for themselves, regardless of what the gender or sexuality of the prospective partner may be.

The last night, a Friday was Cameron's dinner. In spite of the previous late evenings, Cameron was up at six thirty which was a late start for Max but nearer bedtime for Cameron. His shifts at the hotel could result in two or three o' clock finishes. Max was already downstairs cleaning. News had broken in Max's work that Cameron was to appear on the programme and this gave Max almost a local celebrity status by proxy. Colleagues that only gave a perfunctory good morning were now very interested in how things were going and Max, while being equally courteous in return wondered whether part of his private life being made public was such a good idea.

Max had informed his students that he was unable to attend the tutorial on Friday morning due to a domestic situation, a phrase which Max thought worked on several levels. He had approval from his line manager to make alternative arrangements for his classes on the basis that his wife was a devotee of the show. By one o'clock in the afternoon, Cameron had completed his location shoot which involved visiting a local winery. It produced a delicious white entitled 'Cock Hill.' Very easy to swallow, mused Max but only to himself. The camera take of Cameron leaving the house had to be undertaken a second time as that very morning Benson had left a large deposit on the terrace which came into shot. What a critic, thought Max again to himself.

The crew arrived at two. Their immediate admiration for Max's elegant home made Max amenable to them. The first issue was the garden room which ran behind the dining room. The structure was German and the roof a high tech Perspex. The potential for noise if it rained resulted in a suggestion by the producer that bedding be placed on top of the roof.

'Are they seriously suggesting that I go and get one of my Yves Delorme sets and sacrifice it in the name of reality TV?' Max had asked an already stressed Cameron.

'No darling,' Cameron replied with an urgency in his voice, 'they can get some budget range duvets from Tesco.'

Max stared at this idea, pursed his lips and went into his study where he poured a large scotch. It was three pm (thankfully after eight in Japan, he thought). He sat there looking over his tutorials for the following week. They were on the topic of Ultra Vires; companies that act outside their powers. The concept seriously undermined by the Companies Act 1985 and consolidated by the 2006 Act. Max's mind went off on a tangent. In 1880, setting up a company meant that you had one objective and if you entered into a contract outside it, that contract would be void. Companies were restricted so that directors would not utilise investors monies for things other than the company initially represented. Today the opposite was true. Unless a company stated otherwise, the law confirms that a company can trade how it wishes so long as it's legal.

'How much things have altered,' thought Max. 'Today people expect the broadest possible remits in their lives and its called freedom, but invariably this can lead to people taking advantage of others and exposing themselves to pain. Structure was not a bad thing to have in life and reducing power may lead to a better blend in the world,' Max mused to himself.

The crew was very polite and the setting up of the house transformed it quickly from a well researched abode into a set. It seemed far too permanent for Max's liking. By six o' clock, Max realised that this was no longer his home. Fortunately Charlotte had given him an escape and he wondered with a great sense of relief to her large Victorian terrace on Cathedral Road. Benson accompanied, excited by the visitors and by the outing.

Cathedral Road was the spine of Cardiff's centre. Charlotte's home backed onto the park, had six or even seven bedrooms and eluded to the idea that after half an hour, it was unacceptable in a modern home not to have four reception rooms and a forty foot kitchen. The house was a reminder of the days of middle class comfort which included staff, staff that respected their position and were made to feel at home by the owners who were mannered and gracious enough to recognise responsibility.

After a very large gin and tonic, it was Charlotte who began to talk, 'So have you and Cameron got everything sorted for the wedding?' she enquired.

'We're on to it as much as we can,' replied Max, 'but the TV experience has pushed things to one side. It is understandable,' continued Max,' Cameron is excited about the show and we have become the focus of much conversation in work. I really hope he wins, not because of the money, but because he has taken it all so seriously.' Max's mind wondered. He thought about the more amateur shows involving the public, back in the seventies, like The Generation Game. There, amateur meant for the love of it. Sure there were prizes at the end but it represented a spirit of fun that was part of the belief that it was wise not to take things too seriously in life. Today Max thought that the reality TV that he had seen had become all too corporate. People actually became abusive with each other as though TV was now an automatic conduit away from any sense of dignity or manners and everyone's ego was at the vanguard of their own actions. Max loathed this world and hoped that he was not going to see Cameron affected by it.

Max enjoyed being with Charlotte and always opened up when they spoke.

'I was thinking about drugs the other day,' Max decided to break away from the subject of the civil partnership and of the programme. 'Remember drugs Charlotte and my brief encounter?' Charlotte and Marianne had been very supportive after Max's attempted suicide and had been a far greater sense of strength than anyone in Max's own family whom Max felt only enjoyed to see any success in his life.

'You're not taking any?' Charlotte asked with knitted brows and a face that was about to pounce.
'No!' replied Max, a little winded but with a point to make 'I was thinking about what happened to me. I've always believed that drugs should be legalised. I know it now more than ever. Charlotte, it wasn't the drugs that nearly killed me, it was the people with whom I associated while taking drugs that made me vulnerable.' Charlotte listened. Max continued. 'I have seen the parents of teenagers on the TV calling for a stricter policy to be taken on drugs after their child has died, but can we make drugs more illegal than they already are. These people

died even though the drugs were illegal not because they weren't,' Max continued.

'I appreciate what you're saying,' Charlotte began, 'but don't you think it legitimises the drug if it's made legal?' she enquired.

'Yes that's it Charlotte, drugs should be legitimised, that's the only way they can be effectively controlled. Look at my situation two years ago. I was furious with myself for developing a habit but it wasn't that I didn't want to stop that was the problem, it was the fact that the process in which I found need to get the drug was surrounded with criminal associates. It was a highly organised operation and prepared to take action if it did not get its own way, no matter what the cost. The man who held up me at gun point is still walking around with the very same gun, as the police, perhaps understandably, didn't want anything to do with me because I had also broken the law. Yet if the drug had been legal, I would have access to its pharmacology, not to mention the protection of the Sale of Goods Act and I would never have been in a position where someone with a gun would have come to my home. I think I could have got help quicker and avoided the shame of it all.'

Charlotte looked at Max and asked if he wanted another drink. When she sat down again she asked him, 'Max why is this in your head?' Charlotte, like her mother, was a sensitive woman and was one of the few women Max knew who genuinely asked questions about other people to see how they were rather than asking a question as a conduit into telling some corresponding and it was hoped more interesting fact about themselves.

'It's the civil ceremony,' blurted Max, 'I want so much to be married to Cameron but when I look back at what has happened in the last two years I can't believe that I should be here and getting what I really want out of life. It's as if there's going to be a punch line any moment and I'm going to be the butt of the gag.'

'Max,' Charlotte's voice was very soothing,' two years ago you were a mess, a mess with very little support.'

'I had you and Marianne,' declared Max. 'Do you remember?' He then relayed a story about Marianne when Max had been discharged from the hospital. She had brought cake. It was chocolate, and she had also brought cream. There was Simon and Sion as well as Charlotte and Marianne, two very enthusiastic people from a local crisis centre and of course, Max. He had been looking pale after his attempt to end his own life. What possible remedy could there be for him? The others all held their plates with the chocolate cake as Marianne sporting a jug of whipped cream enquired 'Any one wants topping?' Sion, Max and Simon had doubled in laughter and Marianne, without even knowing it, had made Max laugh and had made him strong enough to want to heal and re-engage.

Charlotte's suppers were the envy of everyone. If she had been a contestant on the show now being undertaken at Max's well researched abode she would have won without question. Max marvelled at the way she and Andrew could actually start a meal while their guest were enjoying an aperitif and could produce a pudding, inter course. They were a private couple and Max liked that about them. Their children were Georgie and Tilly and were the most mannered and intelligent children Max had met. He was truly blessed to have such friends he thought to himself, as the most professional looking pasta and home made sauce laced with pine nuts was presented before him. Charlotte and Andrew represented something rare in Cardiff. They could entertain with the best of ingredients and none of the pretentions and their friends felt at home there. How often had Max sat at a dinner table where too much effort was being made. They ate on a large kitchen table which was lost in the top corner of their enormous kitchen.

'Your mother asked me about Basil the other day,' Max told Charlotte.

'Yes she has mentioned the fact you knew each other and believes that Basil holds a torch for you,' replied Charlotte with a giggle.

'Well, it's too late now,' exclaimed Max with a rueful face that broke into a grin.

'Was she unbearable?' asked Charlotte.

'I was a little hurt that she could remain quite so pushy about the idea of Basil and me but I believe your mother is very well intentioned. Perhaps she was after a discount at the salon as an introduction fee. The Dolly Levi of Pontcanna and Llandaff,' said Max with a chuckle.

'She can be insensitive sometimes, she's the same with Andrew and he does so much for her,' admitted Charlotte.

'Yes but you gotta love her,' declared Max, 'and after everything she's been through I'm glad she feels she can still take an interest. I wish my mother would.'

Max then relayed to Charlotte the story of his last visitation to his mother's cottage and they both chuckled like old friends, both concerned about their aging parents, both not completely sure of how a child becomes the parent but both sure that the other would always help if they could, even if it was just exchanging stories. At 11.30 pm, Max conscious that having two little ones meant an early start for Charlotte, bid his adieus and he and Benson walked back to his home.

Max's home was two hundred yards away from Charlotte's and they were connected by a narrow pathway which led through the park. The walk way was lit with intermittent lighting that was essential to ensure the inhabitants of Llandaff were safely deposited out of its more aspirational suburban neighbour. Once on a similar and more intoxicated journey from Charlotte and Andrew's home, Max had come across a young man in a hooded jacket being filated by what appeared at first to be a sleeping bag, until the object lifted its head to reveal a rather plump young woman with a nose ring wearing a padded pink jacket. The two young companions looked very startled when Max interrupted them, inter light space on the park bench, but Max drew upon twenty years of same sex history within him and he waved dismissively,

'Don't mind me,' he had said, 'middle aged gay man returning home, if it goes any further wear a condom, I am a forty per cent tax payer and I don't want to be responsible for your negligence.' Max didn't look back and the moans that he heard coming from the bench declared that his intrusion had had no permanent impact on the jollifications.

Max walked this evening rather more slowly as Benson felt the need to ponder over every piece of debris, both man made, and natural. His stomach felt empty as the gate leading out of the park came into sight. It was a gate important to him as on its inception, he had called the council to inform them that the lack of tarmac around the structure made it almost impossible for disabled access and he felt sure that this was in breach of the law. The council had responded the following day with three builders making the whole device much more user friendly. Max loved that gate and the sense of democratic power it illustrated for him.

Max's home was lit. Blackpool meets Vegas was his first thought and the bill would mean the monthly sky subscription being sacrificed went straight through his mind which had gone on to presume that the incident pending was not over. Respectfully, he turned the key in the door and opened it, as though he was breaking and entering. He noticed one of the crew, a charming yet indie dressed young man called Steve who was enjoying the benefits of under floor heating by lying on his side in the sitting room. Circumspect, Max entered.

'Hello,' he said tentatively to Steve, 'have you finished?'
'We're on pudding,' Steve declared with a slightly weary tone in his voice.
'Is the kitchen safe to enter? enquired Max.
'Yes, they're on a break,' replied Steve.
'I just need to get a few things,' offered Max with Benson now barking at the excitement.

Two of what Max assumed were the other contestants came to the door and fussed over Benson followed by the now matriarchal Sarah fussing the contestants back to the dining room.
'I'm afraid I must be strict,' she declared, 'we're behind schedule.'
'Of course,' said Max, 'I just need a few things from the kitchen.' Max's heart sank. Behind Schedule?

Sarah permitted Max to enter his kitchen to grasp at a bottle of scotch, a glass and a treat for Benson. He left the room and went upstairs. Seeing that both the master bedroom and guest suite were lit with the anticipation of media coverage, he whip stitched it into the dressing room. This had been the master bedroom and still contained a TV. Max felt safe. Benson seemed appeased with the treat.

Max had often fallen asleep with Dawn French. If only she knew, he had thought after Robert had died, that Dawn French in a dog collar would be my bedtime companion the woman would have entered the priesthood for real. This evening seemed no different. Max watched yet another repeat of the Vicar of Dibley feeling safe from all the dangers and perils of the night. There was a sudden knock on the door. It was Cameron.

'Hi Darling,' he said with a smile that made Max want to ask if he would marry him once more.
'Hi,' said Max, 'how are things going?'
'They are finished downstairs and are going to do the results in our bedroom,' replied Cameron.
'So I can come downstairs?' asked Max.
'Yes of course,' answered Cameron.

Excitedly Max ran downstairs to reclaim his estate. In the living room the pending voters were assembled with Steve with whom Max spoke at length about the perils of living in South London on a low income. Max was no expert but he was British and thus could empathise with anyone. Max spoke to a lovely young woman called Claire who had been Monday night, the beach enthusiast and had breast implants.

'Hi,' said Max, 'so you're the one with the false tits, how brave. I've had a lot of plastic surgery and I think it wonderful. Welcome to our home.' He blamed the pasta and not the gin for his gregarious forwardness.

'So you've had surgery?' asked Claire, genuinely interested.
'Oh lots,' declared Max, 'my natural parents are Danny La Rue and Oprah Winfrey. He's dead now though and she never writes.'

Claire laughed until Benson decided she was showing more of her enhancements than anything to which he was used and barked loudly.

'Darling,' Cameron whispered in Max's ear with a reverence that Max remembered from his church days when the vicar had inadvertently got the hymn number wrong and the wardens discreetly updated the congregation as to the correct pre planned number, 'the director has asked that you don't talk to the other contestants.'

'But they're guests in my home,' replied Max.
'Yes but she feels you may be influencing them,' Cameron smiled.
'To what end?' retorted Max, 'I'm not a member of Hare Krishna and with respect that the Neil Canning is worth over £5000. I know you've been to the far east side of the city this week but does everyone think this is the ultimate validation in their existence?' Max was close to another very gay interpretation of Dame Maggie Smith when he saw a sadness in Cameron's eyes.

'Ill retreat upstairs immediately,' said Max and picked up the reticent Benson.

Max again lowered himself into the wicker chair that he had had reupholstered after Robert had sat in it for the last time before he had died in Max's arms. Max and Benson, now in full retreat, treated themselves to a film.

The scotch conveniently placed on the side table just within arms reach.

'Love you my little boy, my beautiful little boy,' Max declared to the unconvinced Benson.

Max switched channels on the TV until he reached 'One Flew Over the Cuckoos Nest.'

'Sympathetic background,' he declared to Benson. Benson replied by yawning and peed against the lamp stand. Oh what the hell, thought Max, the floor's tiled and I'm drunk.

At 6.00 am Max felt a hand gently glide across his face. His eyes opened and he smiled as he saw Cameron.

'The crew have just left,' Cameron said.
'Did you win?' asked Max.
'No, I came last', declared Cameron, 'I blew it.'
'The bunnies?' asked Max
'Yup, the bunnies,' answered Cameron.

Cameron, Benson and Max retreated to the new and make do master bedroom and slept.

Chapter Nine

The following morning which overlapped slightly with the night before was met with a bleary eyed Max pondering the debris, a consequence of the media invasion. The numerous small bottles of still water that littered his once elegant home reminded him of a visit to the 'Heaven' club in London. He had been the designated driver for the evening and stood by the arcade looking on at the revellers with his usual detachment. The beat of the music was heavy yet Max managed to place the tune, 'Tip toe, through the Tulips' in his head and smiled to himself and what would clearly have been reason for him to be extracted from the establishment. There were two men dressed scantily in cages who Max thought looked as though they had done this a lot and seemed jaded. The unattractive ogglers close by, reasoning, Max had thought, that this was the closest they would get to such physical beauty for free that evening. The smell of poppers and the waft of smoke, pre ban, had made for a very sparkling and festive occasion. Suddenly a young man had tapped him on the shoulder.

'Hi mate, would you like something to eat?' he enquired.

'Thank you,' Max had replied, and informed the very slim and florid looking young gentleman that he was full. His friend Peter with whom Max had attended the club and who had taken a more active role in the festivities, had seen the exchange and came over to Max almost immediately after the young gentleman, now looking perplexed had walked off rather abruptly.

'He's gorgeous,' Peter commented.

'Yes,' Max had replied, 'he asked me if I wanted something to eat.' 'I said thank you no, he then walked off.'

'Max!' Peter exclaimed, 'he was asking you if you wanted an e, that's what people take when they drink still bottled water.'

'Well I don't know what he must think I'm on as I told him I was full because we had a McDonalds before we came.' Peter had raised his eyebrows and giggled, while this time Max had looked perplexed.

In front of him this morning, the small bottles seemed disrespectful. The TV crew had left his home at six in the morning and it was now only seven. Max could never sleep in and he could not rest until order had been restored in his home. Three hours later Max thought that his home looked respectable once more and woke a very depressed Cameron.

'Iee got coffee et croissants,' Max said encouragingly with a smile and a bad French accent.

'Thanks my love,' Cameron replied.

'You OK?' Max asked.

'Yea I guess, everything was going so well last night until . . .'

'The bunnies?' interrupted Max.

'Yes, Lucy (a contestant) had just lost her rabbit last week and the idea of eating one didn't go down well. In fact it didn't go down at all. She pushed it around her plate with tears in her eyes' Cameron commented with almost a jadedness in his voice.

'Well I think you're a purist darling and that doesn't always translate well,' Max said in a confirming manner without any authority or references for his evaluation but he felt that it was the right thing to say in the circumstances.

'We have bigger rabbit to fry today anyway,' Max said trying to lighten the mood and failing. 'We have a guest list to compose and I need your help, this is the major political event of the occasion and we can't mess this up, so re caffeinate and bathe and let's get to it.' They had already asked a few close friends if they could attend but there was the need for clarity and thus formal invitations were essential.

Cameron smiled at Max, and was appreciative of the efforts he was making to try and regenerate him from his clear despondency over the previous evening.

'Howard was ghastly,' exclaimed Cameron.

'In what way?' asked Max, knowing the options were numerous.

'He tried to hold things up, would not respond to the director and basically tried to sabotage the whole evening,' Cameron's voice was now full of zeal.

'He went to public school darling, he only knows how to be competitive in a very negative way, it's been ingrained that that's how to succeed in life. Who won?'

'He did, well joint first,' stated Cameron with an air of disdain in his voice. Max wished he hadn't made that last comment about Howard, but too late. He tried again.

'Darling, it really isn't important. You'll get your fifteen minutes and who knows you may get your own show. Bunny boilers,' Max laughed and Cameron, sensing the perspective of the previous evening in the context of the forthcoming events laughed with him.

'Come on darling,' coaxed Max, 'let's get started on the list.'

The Gallery room looked particularly beautiful that morning. The plants gave a jungle like effect as the south facing windows that presented the Garden room allowed the generous sun ample opportunity to fill the narrow and long stretch of space that Max had filled with art, plants and a small breakfast table. The two sat pondering their sure to be controversial decisions over more coffee and chocolate croissants. They smoked. Benson, sensing the occasion decided to stretch out in the sun, looking up occasionally as Max and Cameron reacted to a good idea or a bad idea for a guest. It was Cameron who raised Eliza's name.

'I've agonised over her,' admitted Max, 'we've known each other for over twenty years and she is the most charming company but only when she's sober and I don't think we can guarantee that and when she's drunk so much offence can be caused.'

Max once again relayed to Cameron, the time just after Robert's death when Eliza had called him up, clearly having undertaken her usual Friday evening supper of a bottle of wine and some crisps. This together with several soap operas was considered 'relaxation' time by Eliza but Max knew that this invariably ended with calls to friends sometimes in the small hours of the morning that had no regard for others sleep patterns or feelings. Eliza's call was ostensibly to see how Max was doing but really to glean information on how much Robert had left him.

'I only got the house and contents,' Max had offered, 'the money went to the PDSA.' Yes, just over two hundred thousand had gone to the PDSA and this Max thought would provide sick animals with a high standard of care and kindness. 'They'll all be signed up to BUPA,' he had told Simon, shortly after the contents of the will became known.

'So did you kill him?' Eliza had asked her words had been slurred but clear enough.

'What!' Max had exclaimed, and immediately stood up in his own home with his mobile clenched in his hand like a hawkish barrister furious at Eliza's question. 'I have taken so much care with Robert and I know you're drunk but I really don't need this. How dare you Eliza.' He had decided to hang up on her rather than let rip. He would have said many things he would later regret for sure if he had continued.

The following day Max had left a call from Eliza go to answer phone and when he listened later no mention of the comment was made and she denied it vehemently when Max raised the conversation later. The message had simply asked if he was OK and if she could be of any help she would.

'So she's a no?' asked Cameron.

'I'm afraid so. Your mother is a plain speaking woman and I don't think she would have the same levels of tolerance as we have. Look at last month, I didn't mind going to the hospital after she called me in a frenzy because she had 'broken' her leg but when it was only severely twisted because once again her relaxation evenings had got out of hand, and I helped her back to our home did she really need to pee in the leather chair? I'm just fed up with her victim status. I've tried talking to her about it, but I fear she may be one of those women who presume that their gay friend has all the time and effort in the world for her regardless of his own life. I find it patronising and thoughtless. It's like those women who go to gay bars on a hen night because for them, we're a bloody circus act and it's a story to tell on their wedding day, 'Oh Blodwen, we went to one of those gay bars on Friday, it was a bloody scream. All the men were poofs.' They've banned it in Sydney and I'm not having it here'

'So that really is a no then, with no further issues?' asked Cameron with a grin on his face but his eyebrows raised, rarely being exposed to an actual rant by Max.

'Yes I will tell her it's close family only because of the cost, it's tame but I don't want a confrontation,' said Max almost apologetically.

The two men took another sip of their coffee and Benson re settled himself after the excitement.

'What about our lesbian friends?' enquired Cameron. They had four in total, one couple and one who had been a couple, still lived together and were their well equipped dog enthusiasts.

'Oh yes, now that's another issue. Invite too many and there will invariably be an argument and I may need to get the house insurance changed, invite none and we'll be accused of being exclusive.'

'Who's the best dressed?' asked Cameron flippantly.

'Its much of a muchness darling, the best we can hope for is cleaned and practical,' replied Max smiling at his own ridiculous prejudice.

'Who's the most popular?' asked Cameron.

'The dog handlers, without question. You know Simon and Sion have major issues with the others and again I don't want the day to end in one of those alcohol driven shout offs.' Max had experienced some frightening ones in his home but invited the lesbians to parties because he felt it was the right thing to do. He loathed that gay man/ lesbian split that was openly encouraged by members of both groups.

'The excuse for the other two?' asked Cameron.

'The party line darling, just close family,' said Max as though a Government scandal was being spinned.

Indeed the next issue was family. Cameron's close family consisted of his mother, Lorna and father, Neil, sisters, Jemima and Jillian while Max could only return with mother Einwen, his Aunty Jayne and a cousin from his father's side Nigel, and his partner Anne.

'What about your sister, Angela?' asked Cameron. Max fell quiet.

'Max?' prompted Cameron.

'I heard the question,' replied Max. His face contorted like a sheep which had been fed animal grain with a side order of mint sauce. His lips pursed, the corner of his mouth began to turn down and he made the gesture of looking as though he was giving the idea some serious thought.

'No,' Max said eventually.

Max's sister Angela, had not spoken with Max since he implied that she should have assisted him financially in his hour of need. This had little to do with the fact she was his sister, they had never been similar or close, but more to do with the fact that he and Robert had banked rolled her stay at Max's bungalow, which he had purchased next to his mother's cottage and had been designed for the lucrative holiday lettings market. His sister had split from her husband after it was revealed that she was carrying someone else's child and she and the lover had moved into the newly refurbished bungalow where three months later, her lover had left and had never seen Poppy or Angela since. Max had been told the cottage could fetch eight hundred a week, it was truly beautiful, but Angela only paid one hundred and ninety five pounds a month, half the mortgage payments. After twelve months, Max, much to the consternation of his mother had had to sell the bungalow as it was making a loss.

He and Angela, had different concepts of family. For Max it was an opportunity to help, for Angela, it was an entitlement to take. It was symptomatic of their working class background that she felt this way and believed that life was generally hard for her and thus any opportunity to take had some sort of moral validation attached to it. Max loathed this in people and thought about his conversation the night he had announced his civil partnership to Cameron about attitudes to money. His sister's attitude was viewed with the same disdain and Max did not want her there. She of course had reproduced and had been diagnosed with cancer, the latter was something about which Max had been very upset, but he thought about all the good people in the world that get ill and all the bad people. Illness was not a divine benchmark by which people's characters were judged (he had read Susan Sontag, at her best when discussing the AIDS epidemic) and thus cancer was not something which could change his attitude to people and redeem them, even his sister.

'People got ill because we are living biological beings. That's it,' Max thought to himself.

'OK,' Cameron spoke more with view to guiding the subject away from the issue of family than to just break the now heavy silence in the room. 'Work colleagues.'
'Ah that's easy for me,' said Max with regained enthusiasm in his voice. 'There's Ronald and Roma and Marie and Cameron. Sixteen years in the same place of work and I have two people with whom I enjoy talking and whom I'm sure would enjoy being part of our day. I think in academe that's viewed as an achievement. Two, yes absolutely two. What about you darling?'
'Janet, so one,' replied Cameron.
'Well you've only been working there for three years so I guess proportionately that's much better than I've done,' replied Max.

Cameron had indeed only worked at the hotel for three years and was getting tired of the late hours and the often aggressive guests, a product of the expectation gap Max felt between its marketing and its product. It was a local four star type that was viewed more as a corporate destination than a luxurious one and it was in some need of refurbishment. The heavily patterned wall paper in the bedrooms, the purple and blue and the misplaced dado rail half way up the wall was symptomatic of an eighties style that had dated badly. The hotel had another problem. Its immediate hinterland was a very large and sometimes notorious council estate which used the hotel frequently for wedding receptions. Cameron was in charge of these and on one occasion, was informed by a very buxom prospective bride, that they would have to have the wedding breakfast early and that there was no chance of the evening do being at the hotel as it was beyond the acceptable range for the tagging devices that were worn by about thirty per cent of their guests. The hotel would, as part of the wedding package, offer the bride and groom a free week end's stay on their first anniversary and Cameron would occasionally come home to announce that the bride would love to take advantage of the stay but had asked if she could bring her new partner.

'Such commitment and yet to be fair, honest,' Max had evaluated. 'I wonder what their views are on civil partnerships.' It was one of Max's pense nes moments although he did not wear glasses. He focused again on the list in front of him.

The other guests were friends of either Max or Cameron. Not close friends but close enough for inclusion. This also meant that Howard would be attending the proceedings along with the lovely Caroline and yet four more children.

'So we have eight minors attending,' announced Max.

'You make it sound as though we're going to have an illegal lock in drinking session showing x rated films,' said Cameron.

'No, it's just their status. It's important for the menu and of course, we need to be child friendly at home. Ornaments to the second floor, children's DVD's to be purchased. It's all about management,' concluded Max. 'We don't have children, but I've seen how to pacify them for the greater good of the day.'

Max wondered about some of Cameron's clientele. His views on the occupants of public housing were without prejudice and he often made the observation that people who might be deemed 'hard' or 'rough', 'scrots' (from scrotum) or chavs had a much more accepting attitude to gay people as any positive response was without any intellectual reasoning, which gave the middle classes the appearance of tolerance when in fact deep down Max could often sense they were uncomfortable. Not in public housing, they either liked you or told you to 'fuck off fag' and there was a certain clarity attached to it which Max respected.

The list was now at forty five. Max's personal trainer, Darryl and his wife, Suzanne, friends Benson and Lee, after whom the dog had been named, a lovely unpretending couple that travelled all over the world, and whose stories confirmed many of Max's reservations about such cavalier behaviour. Then there was Leanda and David. Leanda had been a former tenant of Max and now lived in Manchester. Max so hoped she would confirm. Adrian and Michelle, again former tenants and already had confirmed by phone. Max and Lorna, Andy and Chris, Andy and Stuart, Paul and Kirsten. Max read the list to Cameron.

'Pearle and Dean?' Cameron observed. Max laughed.
'Darling,' Max observed, 'are we living the dream here. Nearly all of our friends are couples and there's a seventy five twenty five per cent split in favour of straight people.'
'What do you mean?' enquired Cameron at ease with Max's sometimes over analytical mind.

'Well, it's just so good that with our respective histories we have managed to piece together an almost miniature cross section of society as our friends. All walks of life, within reason, and a really good blend. Legislation against prejudice aside, it's this sort of occasion when we can share with our closest friends and family which is real. I'm proud of this list. I'm proud of our friends and I hope they are proud of us and what we're doing.'

Cameron smiled, 'Darling, I'm very proud of our friends and I'm proud of you, you dope. I'm sure everyone will come, even Howard which is a worthy risk to take. I know what you mean though it's an enormous positive for you that we have such lovely friends.'

'And so many couples. Nearly all of them in fact. Yes it's a normal, special civil partnership. You, me and our wonderful friends.' Max stared at the list which was clearly giving him enormous pleasure to view.

Cameron came over to Max and gave him a kiss on his fore head. Max raised his eyes from the list and brought Cameron closer to him. His slim elegant body, very toned and firm, slid onto Max's lap. They kissed some more and as they did Benson, not wanting to be left out of the moment, jumped between them as if to state his claim in the small family unit. He looked at Max then Cameron and not knowing what to do first, barked loudly and licked them both on the nose.

'Yes Benson,' said Max, its forty six attending and you are the guest of honour.'

Chapter Ten

'No Alan, you're missing my point. I'm saying that marriage is not a romantic concept, not that the ceremony itself shouldn't be romantic. I don't want a dry eye in the house. Man sized tissues will be dispensed at the door. Entry free.'

Max had invited some of the prospective wedding guests for supper, firstly to create a build up to the big day; propinquity now dictating the necessity for a festive atmosphere. Secondly, it was also an opportunity for a group of six gay men to evaluate the recent media coverage of Max's home. He thought about his response to Alan. Before the Civil Partnership Act 2004 had offered legal validation for gay couples, Max had been best man at a gay blessing for a couple who had subsequently been separated by the suicide of one of the partners. He remembered standing there misty eyed as they made a public commitment to each other. Max was crying with emotion, one of the partner's mother was crying from grief and Max's friend Graham was crying because the pollen count was high that day and he had forgotten to take his anti histamines. What a spectacle and the romance in the occasion had been severely tested.

'But Max, you love Cameron and are making a public statement about it, that's a very romantic gesture,' Alan continued. He was one of Max's media friends and an alpha male in every respect. He had been a TV news reporter which meant Welsh TV exposure. In a country where an appearance on TV rendered you a celebrity, Alan remained remarkably self possessed and sensitive. He always challenged Max and Max loved him for this, but he felt that sometimes Alan must think him intellectually tangential and never really appreciated Max's evaluations on subjects which with Alan as a sparring partner ranged from Welsh devolution, of which Max was not in favour, and civil partnerships, of which Max was. He and his actor partner Stephen had been together for ten years. Alan had previously been married, to the more traditional woman and the acrimony he had faced when she discovered that she was not quite the partner Alan needed or wanted had, Max felt, left him scarred.

Timothy Brown

Alan and Stephen lived in a beautiful home which had been exquisitely designed by Stephen, prompting Max to state their dining room, which was a conservatory acting as a conduit between a sitting area and a very elegant kitchen, as the finest space in the city. Tonight as host, he had welcomed them both and they were always such entertaining company. Stephen's actor/model situation was the basis for many work stories and Alan's media career was similarly a source for witty banter and revelations that had to stay, 'between these four walls.' The Lavender Taffia knew years before the Ellen Degeneres appearance that Gareth Thomas was gay and he had universal approval from this small gathering as a man but more importantly as a rugby player. Simon and Sion of course were in attendance and looking very polished and brown after a recent trip to Stiges, which Max felt would be another interesting source for conversation.

'Alan, as you know I love Cameron and I could continue that way without marrying him but this means that if I die, he won't experience any inheritance tax on my estate and will be entitled to my full pension. I can't think of anything romantic about either of those concepts but it places him as number one in my family, and as a gay man, I don't see why when there's a legal opportunity there to create that situation, I should not take advantage of it.' Max thought he had got across his point but Alan replied with an almost cynical tone in his voice.

'Stephen and I have been together now for nearly ten years, we have thought about a civil partnership but it's not necessary.'

'Of course it's not necessary,' replied Max, 'you can achieve most of its consequences through other means such as a will but this is a one stop legal contract that basically covers everything,' Max became almost jealous of his background in law at this point.

'Take the Lorraine Kelly contestants,' Max felt one of speeches cruising through him.

'Contestants?' asked Andy.

'Well that's what they seem like' replied Max. 'There they are on her programme planning how there big day will be, the dress, the church, the flowers, the reception venue, the cake, the registration for wedding gifts and all that jazz. It's all about who can have the best and most imaginative wedding. Has anyone ever asked them whether they are aware that this is the biggest contract into which they will ever enter in terms of property rights? Has anyone taken advice on the affects of section twenty five of the

Matrimonial Causes Act 1973 (as amended)? Does this Act ever get a mention at all? No. Why? Because people and especially women are sold a romantic concept of the wedding and this fronts their whole expectation of the marriage. Martha Stewart has a whole bloody channel dedicated to this idea and she's no advertisement for a successful marriage, Cybil Sheppard acted so.'

Alan and the others laughed at this, they had all seen the bio pic of Ms Stewart and Max had often referenced her in class when trying to explain to a less than enthusiastic group of students about how difficult it was to define and prosecute a case for insider dealing and that Ms Stewart had clearly been unlucky. The prison which subsequently housed her for a while though, Max could confidently report, was wearing matching boiler suits and tabards made with cotton which had an exceptionally high weave count.

'So what you're saying Max, is that you want a romantic wedding but you are telling the world that marriage is not romantic. Do you think Cameron feels good when you say this?' Max looked at Alan. He had a point. Perhaps in his evangelising Max had not been circumspect to Cameron's feeling.

'Alan, Cameron knows I love him and I don't want to detract from the big day but I'm over forty, an officially registered grown up, I hope. I just want to make it clear to people that I'm going into this with my eyes open and my knowledge complete. That, I believe, should make me a man who is responsible enough for marriage. Anyway I believe that there is a media conspiracy against marriage,' Max announced.

'Really,' Alan replied, 'and what makes you think that?'
'Well,' replied Max trying not to grin. 'Ms Kelly gets them in first in the morning and makes them all fuelled up on the idea that their future will be all so romantic once they have married. The marriage then runs out of steam, when they realise that the ceremony and hype misrepresents the reality and responsibility that follow. The husband has an affair after meeting a childhood sweetheart from school, on Facebook. He gets her pregnant, his wife gains five stone and starts wearing leggings. She smokes like an industrial chimney in Delaware and they all end up on the Jeremy Kyle show two years later having a paternity test. I tell you it's a conspiracy to achieve watchable TV. It's all your fault.' By this time Max and the others were laughing.

'Your right darling,' said Alan, touching Max on the arm with a 'there there' it's time for bed expression on his face, 'it's all my fault.' Realising the tease, he lent over and gave Max a kiss on the cheek. He and Stephen were a handsome couple and Max smiled at the way Alan defused the conversation. Max was so happy to have this evening with the 'boys'. It was an alternative to a stag night which Max felt was for younger people who did not have a tracker mortgage.

Cameron turned to Sion at this point, 'So how was Stiges, after the false start?'

'Oh don't,' replied Sion, 'I can't believe we over slept and missed the plane and we had to drive to the airport in Bristol, which as you know is tucked inconspicuously down a lane so that know one can find it, just to re book for the following day. It was a bloody nightmare, I'm sure that airport is an ex training complex for MI5 that's why you have to drive through Bedminster to get there. Bloody Bedminster, I mean who builds an airport next to a Morris dancing pole? I thought we were in Devon at one point until we saw a minute sign saying airport, first left after you see Farmer John milking Maisey the cow. Don't beep your horn she's in season.' Sion's dry execution of Simon and his mishap caused the group to belly laugh. Sion was a quietly spoken man with a beautiful soft, educated Welsh accent. The most unpretending of individuals he demanded universal respect having the ability to comment on the issue of anything just by re stating the facts. A very clever skill Max had observed. He was a dignified man and Simon's greatest asset. Max and Cameron loved him.

'We went into a bar,' Simon declared.
'Well I should hope so, it's a gay Mecca,' observed Max.
'It had a room,' continued Simon looking increasingly serious.
'Simon, are you OK?' asked Max.
'It had a bath in it,' continued Simon, 'and no plug.'

As Simon relayed the encounter with the bath his eyes looked left and right quickly as if to ensure that someone from the anti gay neo-nazi policing force could not over hear what he was saying.

'So you went into a fetish bar where you discovered a toy room with a facility in it for guys who enjoy golden showers, is that right?' Max enquired with an air of experience in such matters which belied his past if not his curiosity.

'Eeewww!' exclaimed Simon.

'So how did you manage that?' asked Max with far too much curiosity in his voice.

'Well Sion and I went for a drink before dinner and we noticed this bar with a rainbow flag in the front. We hadn't tried it before but it had very interesting detailing on the facade so with my architect's eye, I wanted to see if it was replicated inside. We wandered in and ordered some drinks then we noticed four men in the corner all stood in a circle. When we looked closer we saw a fifth man who was kneeling in the middle providing the four with shall we say oral relief.' The others were in fits of laughter by this time as Simon's face went crimson.

'What did you do love?' Max asked with a comforting pat on Simon's arm.

'Well the drinks were ten euros, two Christmas gins and tonics, so we thought well we're not rushing these and the dinner table was booked for forty five minutes later so we decided to air on the side of discretion and go into the 'lounge' area, except it wasn't a 'lounge' area at all, but a play room with all sorts of accoutrement,' Simon continued with a hand gesture to the throat suggesting that someone had stolen his pearl necklace.

'There was a bath, and an X cross with ties on the corner, a cage and a sling,' Simon stated.

'Great detailing then,' Alan observed.

'Did you try anything on for size,' Max enquired winking at Cameron.

'Hell no, two of the sports team from the scrum in the other room had followed us in so we whip stitched it back to the bar. I didn't spill a drop but my slice of lime ended up on the floor,' Simon concluded proudly.

Fits of hysterical laughter followed as Simon's final double entendre was fully digested. The trip had clearly been successful for the happy couple and they were as ever such an asset to have at the dinner table but the thought of such a wrong turn even in one of Spain's chicest resorts made Max realise that it was probably better holidaying in Cornwall.

'It's so expensive now in Stiges since the pound has gone down against the euro, it's at least twenty per cent dearer than it was a year ago' Simon evaluated, 'but it's also so elegant there. The beach is beautifully prepared each day and you are provided with tables and chairs which you can hire and just to sit on the beach, it's all very civilised.'

'That's why it's such a haunt for gay men,' observed Max. Look at the UK, all the best cruising areas are in smart, middle class parks. Hampstead Heath, Hyde Park, even Pontcanna Fields in our own beloved Cardiff. 'Its all very smart arsed indeed.'

'What about Clapham Common?' asked Alan in his usual challenging tone.

'Well its south of the river, but its expensive to live there. I once had a mature student whose mother had bought a house there in nineteen forty eight after all the snow, overlooking the park. When she wanted to sell, her three thousand pound investment was worth nearly eight hundred thousand pounds and the family wanted my advice on inheritance tax issues. It's very up and coming there,' replied Max.

'I think that's exactly the point darling,' countered Alan.

'So how was the cooking contest?' Stephen asked Cameron, with all the others concurring that they wanted to know.

'Well I came last,' replied Cameron with his lips turned down and an exaggerated look of depression on his face.

'Oh love never mind,' replied Stephen with a mellow hint of his Yorkshire accent adding sincerity. 'These programmes are all fixed. I was in a programme years ago where the winner became an entertainment's officer on board ship. There was a gay manager with a bulb head who said that my introductions were too embroidered. I've worked at Glyndebourne and the West End and the bloody idiot's head was so far up his own arse there wasn't room left for a reasonable opinion. A young girl got the job which was fine, she was very good, but it shows that anything that requires an opinion to get a result is unpredictable. Don't worry love I'm sure your cooking was excellent, this fish pie is.' Stephen was very sweet about the whole media event and Cameron blushed with gratitude.

'So who won?' asked Alan.

'Howard,' replied Cameron. 'He tied with one of the other women.'

'Howard?' asked Alan. 'What Howard from the Bay?'

'The very same,' replied Cameron as Alan's eyes widened.

'When did you hear he was on the programme?' Alan asked.

'The night before the first dinner,' replied Cameron.

'And he'd not mentioned it before?' Alan asked.

'Not once, no,' replied Cameron. 'He said that the team had been badgering him for weeks.'

'That's nonsense,' stated Alan with such an air of authority, no one would have challenged him. 'There are people queuing up for these reality programmes, who does he think he is, Brad Pitt?'

'He was quite awful,' Cameron confessed, 'and the director had had quite enough of him by the end of the evening. How it will go down at his school I don't know. Any aspirations he had about being discreet over his sexuality were well and truly blown. I don't know what the head of governors is going to think.

'Who is he?' asked Simon, 'Helen Keller? That man is as gay as a badger.'

'A badger?' Max asked.

'They always build a nice toilet somewhere away from their set, so as to keep up hygiene standards, how gay is that?' Simon replied.

I feel apprehensive about him coming to the wedding,' Cameron said with a reflective tone in his voice.

'He's coming to the wedding?' Alan looked at Max and waited for a comment.

'I know, he's a former lover but he's also an old friend and he's bringing Caroline and the kids so it's strategic. He's not all bad Alan,' Max offered.

'No, true but he has clearly upset Cameron,' replied Alan with a defensive tone in his voice.

'He was drunk,' Max said.

'No excuse,' Alan replied.

'I know but the invitation has been extended and we are not taking it back, you will have to be chief gay man with issues handler I'm afraid. It's an unpaid position but we will guarantee to love you forever, even if you marry another woman.' This time it was Max's turn to lean over and kiss Alan who smiled and promised he would do all he could but could not rule out physical violence as a control mechanism.

'So love, what did you cook? Stephen asked.

'Rabbit,' replied Cameron as his face crunched suggesting a huge faux pas.

'And they were vegetarians?' asked Stephen.

'No,' replied Cameron, 'but one of them was clearly a fully paid up member of the Bright Eyes and Bobtail club and did not appreciate bugsy on the plate.'

'Well love, it seems you just had some bad luck and bad guests. You're a bloody great cook.'

From Stephen this was an enormous compliment. Like Charlotte, he was very accomplished in the kitchen and Max marvelled at all the ingredients that were on display in his home. Max wondered if there was a Harry Potter styled three and three quarter aisle at Tesco where Stephen purchased such things. Before he met Cameron Max had felt that eating at Alan and Stephen's home always made him feel hugely inadequate in that reciprocity would be a somewhat mitigating experience. Thankfully Cameron could cook and his friend's sincere generosity that evening went a long way in healing the painful media experience.

'So,' Max changed the subject, 'You two won't be returning to Stiges for a while I presume.' Sion and Simon fell quiet.

'We've booked for next August already,' replied Simon.

'Why?' asked Max.

'The hotel we liked was fully booked in July,' replied Simon and the six friends laughed uncontrollably.

'We have got you a present for your civil ceremony,' Stephen announced.

'Oh that's wonderful,' Max replied genuinely over whelmed. He had acquired so many things over the years and knew it would be difficult to buy gifts for him and Cameron, they had so much china, clothes and other domestic comforts. It was a problem for a committed guest at the wedding of a middle aged gay man.

'I'm going to paper that wall in your sitting room,' announced Stephen.

'Oh that's wonderful!' replied Max, genuinely moved. 'We have purchased the paper already in anticipation but we didn't like to ask you because you have been so busy of late,' Max confessed.

'Well I hope it helps,' Stephen offered very self effacingly. Max and Cameron knew his skills around the home and the cost of the paper warranted an expert. They were truly touched by the offer.

'I'd like to propose a toast,' declared Cameron. 'To our civil partnership and our ability to choose such wonderful friends.'

The small, happy gathering all stood and wished Max and Cameron all the very best. Max's eyes misted for a moment. The dining room had worked its magic again. His beloved peer group, so generous, so kind and amusing they were accomplished men who seemed genuinely happy about the ever closer civil partnership.

Chapter Eleven

'We'll get a marquee and put that in the garden!' Cameron stated with an air of authority, a product of the past three years making helpful suggestions to men and women whose idea of an elegant marriage included pink balloons, goldfish as centre pieces on the wedding breakfast table and too much cleavage displayed by the bride.

'A marquee in our garden!' exclaimed Max, 'do they make them that small?' He sized up the space, which was immaculately kept behind his well researched abode. It currently held some pots and a table that sat ten and the thought that anything aspiring to be a marquee would result in a far more inclusive contribution to the festivities from at least two or even three of his neighbours.

'A *gayzebo* then,' offered Cameron, 'but with sides.'

'We'll call it a gazebo then. That's fine so long as I know what I'm googling,' replied Max.

Within two hours and exposure to a variety of gazebos ranging from a tent to a holiday cottage, Max had successfully purchased a white plastic gazebo which was a perfect match for the modest terraced area. It was deemed luxurious by the suppliers, a word clearly over used in the marketing strategies for, inter alia, apartments which only had to include an en suite, and hotels, which only required a trouser press. To justify their concept of luxurious, the suppliers of the gazebo had honed in on the fact that this particular one had windows detailed into the sides, giving the effect of a celestial Wendy house on steroids but size mattered on this occasion.

'We'll be able to look through that and see the wall,' Max commented conscious of the irrelevance of the feature.
'We can modify it,' Cameron suggested.
'To the point where it's not recognisable,' replied Max.
'Some ribbon and a chandelier,' Cameron was clearly on a roll with his thought process.
'Ill get three hundred meters of white and yellow,' offered Max. Cameron smiled and rolled his eyes.

'Don't forget we have to be at the Registry Office today to pay the deposit and confirm the music,' Max called as he googled ribbon and more optimistically anything that suggested how to hide a twenty foot gazebo in the garden.

'What time?' Cameron asked.

'One o'clock,' replied Max, as Benson jumped onto his lap, took one look at a picture on the computer of a gazebo adorned with lace netting, pearl strings and ostrich feathers and gave out a very large yelp.

'It's OK my boobbie,' Max looked in earnest at the style critic now licking his nose, 'daddy won't be going down that path.'

At one o' clock, Max had parked his car outside City Hall which dominated Cardiff's civic centre and confirmed to anyone with any doubt, this was the capital of Wales. It was a beautiful white building built on the success of the ports and heavy industry which had characterised the city during the nineteenth century. Max and Cameron walked into the office where a variety of baby carrying women and rather sad looking people represented the fact that they were in the births, marriages and deaths section.

Max remembered registering Robert's death at the old office four years prior and thought how uncivilised the whole experience is when you loose a loved one. Their purpose today was to give notice of their civil ceremony which required at least fifteen days between the signing of the notice and the ceremony itself.

'We are here for an appointment to give notice for our civil partnership, Dr Hubbard-White and Mr Stewart,' Max informed the very nonchalant young woman who sat drinking a mug of coffee behind the desk. 'How rude,' Max thought.

'Yea, you're with Mr Jeffries in room six. What it is, you go down the corridor and the room is on the right.'

'What it is?' Max thought to himself. He had observed this idiosyncrasy in the language of people from Cardiff and its environs for some time. He wondered why people felt the need to preface their conversations with the phrase.

Mr Jeffries was an affable gentleman who seemed genuinely pleased to see Max and Cameron.
'Have we met?' he asked Max. Indeed they had.

'I did a reading at a civil partnership three years ago, and we spoke,' Max offered. The three men sat down and the appropriate forms were taken out of a large grey filing cabinet.

'You realise we have no vacancies in the registry office on the 7th yes?' Mr Jeffries bomb shell froze Max and Cameron in their seats.

'No,' Max broke the silence, 'we did not know this.' His mind suddenly thought of all those hand written invitations that would now require an amending telephone call.

'Of course there is a registrar available, Mrs Robinson, but you will have to hire one of the state rooms upstairs.'

'Coo coo ka choo' thought Max.

'It's three hundred pounds for the hire of the Old Council Chamber which is our most popular venue,' Mr Jeffries continued. Max saw his honey moon budget immediately mitigated and then slashed completely when the kindly civil servant stated:-

'Of course the added cost will be that you will have to pay a further three hundred and seventy five pounds for the registrar to visit,' Mr Jeffries explained. Regardless of whether it's upstairs in the same building or ten miles away in a designated social club, there was a flat fee for a registrar who worked outside the registry section.

'So we pay the city three hundred and seventy five pounds for Mrs Robinson to walk up a flight of stairs?' Max wanted this confirmed such was his disbelief.

'Yes, I'm sorry,' Mr Jeffries exhaled deeply as he said this, 'but that's the policy.'

Max did the maths in his head and concluded that only Kate Moss earned more money for walking such a short distance but they really had little choice in the matter.

Max read over the forms, which required a thirty three pound fifty fee, per person, for the civil partnership registration notice.

'Per person?' Cameron enquired, 'do people actually come here alone?'

Mr Jeffries, the consummate professional smiled but ignored Cameron's evaluation that the form really didn't make complete sense. They both read further.

Max became pensive. The questions asked if either of them were already married and were they UK nationals, all very predictable and understandable. It was the questions about his family background that had made him quiet. What is the current occupation of your father? Max thought for a moment. He hadn't seen his father in over twenty years and even though the man would only be in his late sixties, Max wasn't sure if he was alive or dead. He had thought about his father a lot after his parents divorced when he was only fourteen but over the years, the pain of that marriage and the abuse were placed far away in Max's mind. For him though, having seen a talented and handsome man become an unloving husband and negligent parent was an inspiration. He had seen those roles done badly and the consequential suffering it caused. He would never be that person. His civil partnership would work and he would be the commensurate partner to Cameron and dad to Benson.

Max's 'coming out' to his father had sparked a most unusual development in their relationship. At first, his father had been supportive and had made all the right noises about Max being his son and that he would love him whatever. That was nearly twenty five years ago and Max was seventeen. Then however came Allister. Max was nineteen when he met him at club in Bristol. Allister had been stood by a piano and Gerard, who had been, as usual, Max's companion for the evening, spotted him.

Allister had enjoyed Max's awkwardness and the two were soon lovers. Even now he remained one of those bitter sweet memories for Max who had in a very immature way, fallen in love. Their relationship had lasted six months during which time, Max's own insecurities about such a beautiful man choosing him had resulted in Allister ending the relationship leaving Max broken. It was all so long ago now and the pain was over. Max had found love as a grown up and here he was pledging his commitment to a man he truly loved.

It was his father's reaction to Allister that still made him thoughtful. He had resented him from the first moment they met and led eventually to his father rejecting both Allister and Max. Max wondered if it was jealousy or just that his father had not realised that being a gay man actually resulted in concepts like boyfriends or partners turning up. Whatever the reason, Max had never seen his father since and was surprised by the feelings that rose within him when faced with having to think about the man.

Max wondered at his relationship with his father. It was something the feminists could never judge or understand, but the validation a father can give a son and the subsequent insecurities that arise when that is not forthcoming is probably the most pivotal development for a young man. Max had experienced rejection from his father and it had taken years for him to appreciate that he could be loved for the man he was. He had experienced it with Robert, yes, but he had had it confirmed with Cameron.

A surge of strength came through Max as he signed the form leaving the part about his father with an UNKNOWN in bold across it. This was quite acceptable to Mr Jeffries who confirmed that many people came before him who did not know the whereabouts of their own parents. Max felt labelled but it soon passed.

Mr Jeffries then made a call to the functions office which was situated on the mezzanine level in the main entrance hall. Max and Cameron were led by the now warm and chatty Mr Jeffries along the main corridor where Max noticed the portrait of His Royal Highness, the Prince of Wales, painted by Max's friend David. David had painted a somewhat revealing yet tasteful nude of Max at the same time as the portrait of the heir to the throne and Max had giggled with David afterwards at the idea of any mix up in the delivery of the two portraits.

'They'll raise the council tax, if my backside gets displayed in city hall,' Max had wailed much to the amusement of his very accomplished artist friend.

They were met half way up the stairs by a very elegant woman called Mrs Price-Thomas. Max loved the welsh concept of putting two very ordinary surnames together in order to create one that aspired to be more elegant. It suited her.

'Hi, I'm Gail Price-Thomas, and I'll be showing you some of the rooms we have available. You'll be pleased to know that all the rooms are available on the 7th August.' In view of the costs involved this came as no great surprise to Max.

'How many guests?' Mrs Price-Thomas asked.
'About fifty,' Cameron replied.
'Well I don't think you'll want the main room as it seats nearly five hundred and it's fifteen hundred for the afternoon,' Mrs Price-Thomas said much to Max's relief that they were not going to experience the same pressure selling he had experienced in his now much lamented trips to New Bond Street.

Max had been to a Mardi Gras Ball in the main reception room about six years prior. Cardiff had been an interesting mix that day, with Wembley Stadium being refurbished, the play offs for the football leagues were hosted at the Millennium Stadium which attracted amongst others a lot of northern people who seemed to have a very relaxed attitude to matching attire and a penchant for shell suits.

'I didn't know they were still being made,' Max had observed to Stephen and Alan with whom he had attended the ball.

'It keeps out the cold,' Stephen said, an authority due to his own background, 'and they are easy to wipe off stains' The three saw a surprisingly happy mixture of drag queens and football supporters walk down St Mary's Street as they sat in an open top BMW with pink carnations on their left lapels. There was some confusion caused by the fact that a few of the football supporters were skin headed and wore tight jeans but again Stephen could report that this constituted practical fashion with a view to looking tough.

'But they look so gay,' Max observed. 'I guess for them this is abroad, and it will be just another reason to undermine the Union.'

Mrs Price-Thomas broke Max's reminiscences. 'How about we look at the Old Council Chamber first, get a feel of the place?
'Great idea,' Max replied.

As they continued up the broad stair case towards the first floor Max saw the imposing and evangelising statue of St. David himself. On the night of the Mardi Gras ball he had been fashioned with a pink feather bower. Today he looked much more sanctimonious and, Max thought, appropriate. The marble stone used for the columns and the balustrades gave the most glamorous effect. Max was proud this belonged to his city.

Mrs Price-Thomas led Max and Cameron into a dimly lit foyer which belied the subsequent detailed beauty of the chamber. It, like Max's dining table, was circular obviously affording the same type of comforts for those who wished to engage in debate about city life and budgets. It was an ornate room with oak panelling and a truly magnificent rococo styled chandelier. The seats suggested individuality and were padded with a very rich green leather. It was gay with gravitas, thought Max and he quickly confirmed that this room would be most suitable. Max looked over at Cameron, whose eyes had misted.

'Hey darling,' Max placed a comforting arm around Cameron's shoulder. 'We can't break down on the day.'
'It's so beautiful,' Cameron observed. At that moment, Max realised that any respect for budget was inconsequential to the look of joy on his partner's face. It was to be their room without doubt and would be of no value to anyone that day except them. Mrs Price-Thomas, sensitive to such an emotional situations gently asked, 'Have you thought about the music?'

Max took out a list containing, Pachelbel's Canon and Gigue, for the walk in or procession as it was referred to by Mrs Price-Thomas. Then Maria Callas singing 'La Mamma Morta,' from Giordano's opera 'Andrea Chenier', for the signing of the register. Its gay pedigree and thus suitability for the occasion, came from its inclusion in the film Philadelphia, but Max afforded himself a smile when the couple had chosen it. 'It means 'They Killed My Mother,' he had told a very amused Cameron.

'And to proceed out?' Mrs Price Thomas was now very officious as she would be in charge of executing their choices.

'Saint Saens Organ Symphony Number Three,' replied Max.

'The theme music from 'Babe' replied Cameron at the same time.

They were all popular pieces that would not tax any of their guests and Mrs Price-Thomas gave a nodding of approval for the choices. Max and Cameron were then shown two other rooms but they did not compare with the idiosyncratic beauty of the chamber.

They paid the deposit and were allowed to see that their names had now been booked for the room on the computer just in case, Max thought, they had not anticipated being trusted to do it. Max and Cameron had experienced council administrators in relation to their respective council tax bills and appreciated the gesture. Excitedly and with some relief that the events of the 7th were piecing together Max and Cameron got into the car and reflected on the events of that afternoon. It was a warm July day. The formal park behind city hall was punctuated with students and other young people who were taking full advantage of the space.

'It's going to be so perfect,' exclaimed Cameron with a sigh.
'I'm marrying you,' replied Max with his eyes misting.
'The chamber is an amazing space,' reflected Cameron.
'It will be an amazing day,' replied Max.

As the traffic around the castle began to build with the pending rush hour, the two men felt cocooned in the purring car and they smiled at each other. The day was coming closer when they would walk proudly down the aisle and declare their civil partnership. It was a happy time indeed.

Chapter Twelve

'Place the pole marked four into the pole marked two, it says so there I'm not lying.'

Max and Simon were attempting to erect the gazebo. Simon had offered his services as he and Sion had been extended the position of supporters on the wedding day and they responded with much affection and offers of help. The task in question was typical of the expectation gap between manufacturer who presumed a detailed and professional understanding in erecting by the consumer and the consumers who were having erecting dyslexia on this occasion.

'Four into two Simon,' Max confirmed with an added pointing of his index finger on to the now depressingly entitled 'picture one' of the instructions. The two friends had been busying with the less than luxurious 'tent' as

Max had referred to it for over an hour and it still seemed to be eluding their joint abilities to erect.

'Wait a minute,' Simon interjected, 'we're making the roof first aren't we?'
'Yes,' replied Max, 'why?'
'Oh I thought it was odd to have a piece going down the middle on the floor. That's why I thought this couldn't possibly be right. Oh I'm so sorry, we'll do it in no time now.'

True to his words and with Max repressing the desire to sack Simon on the spot, the friends fully erected the gazebo within twenty minutes. Sion and Cameron were inside taking the much more sensible option of cleaning the garden room. It was three in the afternoon and the ceremony was only a week away.

'A drink I think Simon,' announced Max once their labours were completed.
'A stiff one,' replied Simon laughing at the amount of times the two had referred to their erecting problems within a ninety minute period.

As if on cue Cameron and Sion appeared at the back door with a pitcher of Pimms. The jug contained several varieties of fruit decorating its base while the inviting amber coloured fluid lifted everyone's spirit.

'Simon did not want to fit four into two!' Max exclaimed, 'that's been the problem.'

'Love he can't manage with fractions,' Sion replied much to the amusement of Max and Cameron. Simon's lips pursed but he grinned enjoying the completion of the reception room now looking conspicuous in Max's garden. The plastic was a little creased and you could not really see out of its windows but it provided cover in the event of the unpredictable summer weather.

'That was difficult,' Simon stated as he took his first sip of the Pimms.

'It's a wise man that knows his limitations Simon but it's a happy man who is at ease with them,' Max replied.

'Where's that from?' Simon asked.

'The first bit is Socrotes,' Max confirmed, 'but I added the last bit. I think once we were over the initial prejudice about the instructions we did very well. It looks dreadful but useful.'

'I have an addition,' Simon announced.

'We know dear,' Max replied, 'and we're so happy for you, for you both.'

'I'll just get it from the car,' Simon said, and he skipped off into the house being chased by a very intrigued Benson who had already launched the new addition in the garden with a christening pee against one of the main poles.

Five minutes later Simon returned walking very slowly and carefully, like an acolyte in a catholic mass. In his arms stretched almost full to accommodate its size, was an ornate chandelier.

'Good Lord!' exclaimed Max annoyed for taking the Lord's name in vain but truly astonished by Simon's addition. 'Did you raid Liberace's coffin?'

'You don't like it?' asked Simon.

Max pursed his lips, frowned, pursed again, frowned again. His bottom lip then fell slightly open and his eyes widened. Locally this gesturing was referred to as Swansea lip and Aberdare eye.

'It's unique. Yes, I think I can safely dub it the most unique item I've ever seen,' replied Max.

'It's amazing,' Cameron observed. He began looking more closely at the chandelier which dazzled in the afternoon sun. Benson was confused at the item and for any purpose it may have and decided to rechristen the tent, looking very wary of the whole tableau in front of him.

'It's certainly a conversation piece, Simon but what will we do with it?' Max asked.

'It'll go in the middle of the gazebo,' Simon replied and held it aloft in the middle of the tent. Max observed for a moment and concluded that it could not detract from the construction and was further won over by the fact that the entire item was made of sturdy plastic.

'So the focal point of our reception will be a plastic chandelier that has been taken straight from the set of 'Les Cage Aux Folles?' Max concluded. 'Perfect!'

'You don't have to use it,' Simon said a little hurt at the coolness of Max's reception of the lighting device.

'Darling it's wonderful, I love it,' Cameron said.

'OK then of course we'll use it. Let's try it out,' Max stated and gave Simon a little hug of appreciation. 'It was just a shock Simon, I think it will work well. Thank you,' Max said. The chandelier was attached to one of the poles entitled four and connected to the garden plug which was placed conveniently and discreetly by the raised border. As the chandelier was lit, even in the mid afternoon sun, it provided a glamorous and uplifting centre piece and detracted from the short comings of its host. The four friends looked on for a long while. Benson concurred.

'Yep, it's perfect,' Max admitted and he smiled to himself. His prejudice had been usurped by Cameron's enthusiasm and this he knew was one of the most important reasons for their union. Cameron had an energy about him that was infectious and it made Max stronger and more at ease with life and with people.

'So what are you two wearing next Saturday?' Max asked Sion and Simon.
'Oh we wanted to talk to you about that,' Simon replied. He and Sion fell silent for a moment and Max was confused about their reticence to answer the question.
'We were thinking waist coats,' Simon offered.
'Lovely,' replied Max.
'With jeans,' announced Simon.

The glorious summer sun, now bathing the rear garden with its mellow five o clock warmth suddenly seemed mitigated by this news. Max remained stoic but to the point in his reply.
'We have invited lesbians to the civil ceremony but we weren't thinking of making them a theme,' offered Max,

with both Swansea and Aberdare written all over his face. 'Can you elaborate on the type of jeans?' Max asked.

'They're very smart with some beautiful detailing on the side of the knee,' Simon was grinning at this point but Max knew he was not joking about the denim attire.

'Well my dear we have been friends for a long time so I won't judge and at least it's not satin blouses with Magyar sleeves,' Max said truly winded by the announcement. He took another large sip of the Pimms which settled him a little.

'We thought that if we were smart but understated, it would enhance you,' Sion offered in his usual charming way. Max reflected on this for a moment and decided uncharacteristically to bend to the warmth of the afternoon sun and fane pacified by the explanation. 'It might even work,' he thought to himself, 'and we can wear matching dungarees.'

'So what are you going to do about your names?' Simon asked.

'Well we're keeping Max and Cameron,' Max scoffed still thinking about the jeans and their subsequent appearances on the wedding photographs. Max had already personified the garments and was convinced they had ASBOs. 'We have thought about the surnames. Hubbard-White-Stewart, suggests we have married into the British royal family and we don't want to misrepresent ourselves being a couple of queens,' Max joked. 'Then there's Stewart-White but that sounds like a christian and surname and White-Stewart sounds like an advert on a racist dating site so we were thinking Hubbard-Stewart. Of course I won't change it at work because people will wonder who I am and as I'm not a woman, no one will have the expectation that I would ever change my name. I don't think society has got its head around that yet and I don't want to confuse,' Max said with some sincere generosity in his voice.

'Yes I think that trips nicely,' Simon replied. He and Sion had the advantage of Tomassi and Turner as their surnames which Max had thought was another good reason for them to enter a civil partnership.'

'Of course it doesn't happen automatically for us,' explained Max. 'We shall have to execute a deed of change of name which is an added expense. It's not a priority but we are thinking about it.'

The four friends sat in silence. The garden looked so different. The table had been taken with surprising ease to the car port and Max's beloved BMW was relegated to the street, much to his concern. The gazebo was sized by the four men each generating improvements for it with differing imaginative skill. Some time and deep reflection passed before Cameron offered the first suggestion.

'We can place ribbons around the poles in the four corners and along the top of the sides. Then some net in bows on the four internal corners and of course flowers. I can make it look amazing,'

Max's love for Cameron and the afternoon sun did not mellow his disbelief that the device in front of them could reach such dizzy heights of beauty but he was charmed by his partner's enthusiasm suggesting that it should all be done very Doris Day in yellow and white. They all agreed the scheme and Simon suggested fairy lights around the door of the garden room. 'They'll act as a conduit,' he evaluated with a smirk on his face. Simon always had a conduit for every occasion. That and canter lever were two words which defined him as an architect.

'Conduit and canter lever, I know you, if we have one we'll have to find the other,' Max joked to his accomplished friend.

'He gets one of them into every conversation,' confirmed Sion.

'Oh shut up,' replied Simon smiling, 'I'm a pro.'

'Yes with a wonderful addition and the ability to erect . . . eventually,' Max commented.

'So the tables and chairs are arriving on Wednesday, the cutlery and crockery Thursday evening and the wine, Friday afternoon. We have the rings, the clothes, the room booked, the photographer, the caterer, the guests, arrangements for guests to stay at a local hotel, and next week booked off work.' Max's list was he thought quite complete. He wanted no one staying at the house because being host and groom was too pressured and it spoiled the sense of occasion.

'What about favours?' asked Cameron.

'Favours?' the other three asked together.

'The bride and groom at a lot of weddings, place little gifts on the table as a way of saying thank you for coming. It's a little gesture,' Cameron continued.

Max had experienced this at a friend's wedding three years prior. The gift was a lottery ticket and he had won ten pounds. He suggested this as the cost would be reasonable.

'That's a great idea but what happens if someone wins the millions? asked Simon.
'We claim and equitable trust over the proceeds as we purchased them.' Max replied jokingly but not without the thought lingering in his mind for a while. 'I'll check the case law on that first,' he continued.

The others laughed at the ease with which Simon could always make Max a little pensive. The two couples always ended up laughing over their lives. They were all accomplished. Not high-flyers but definitely a dual carriage way somewhere nice in the country. The night drew in gently and the Pimms jug refilled several times. It all looked so real now as Max stared at the changes the day's labours had made to his garden. 'Only one more week,' he thought and smiled.

Chapter Thirteen

The work/life balance in the week leading up to the civil ceremony left Max with a constant feeling of angst. When he worked, he worried about the ceremony and reception, when he prepared for the ceremony he thought about his work. He loved lecturing in law and had been informed by many, but not all, of his students that he was good. His end of year feed back forms were on the whole a joy to read and he was sensitive to criticism in this area. It was his passion for knowledge, and for trying to encourage intellectual curiosity that motivated him. 'You've heard of the X factor?' he would ask his students, 'well here we deal with the 'why' factor.' Restate facts gets you a solid 2:2 but evaluate, analyse, hypothesise and synthesise and the sky is the limit,'

It's funny though how one small random event can upset the already strained balance in an individual and for Max it was the receipt of his quarterly Tesco club card vouchers. The vouchers were a product of a points based system which Max felt sure was something akin to the immigration process, as the recipient earned more and more points as he or she shopped. Cigarettes were excluded from the reward system which Max found fascistic but he remained circumspect about the policy. It was usually a delight to get the vouchers.

When he opened the envelope he was anticipating about fifty pounds as he and Cameron shared the one card and all their shopping for food and petrol was with the store. They had over five thousand points as a result of the double points system. It read, 'Thank you for your loyalty, here is twenty five pounds.'

'Darling,' Max called for assistance from Cameron.
'Yes,' Cameron came running as Max's tone suggested something was amiss. 'Only twenty five pounds, have I missed something?' He showed Cameron the booklet containing the one twenty pound voucher and the one five pound voucher.
'Ah here it is, you have to double these in store where you will get a token for the following areas: baby clothes;

useless, fashion items; inappropriate, ah flowers. That's useful, we'll get the flowers.'

Max felt a little annoyed that the doubling capacity was limited to certain areas in the store. He had often noticed the heterosexual bias in the sirloin steak section. He had told his neighbour Michaela, 'You get one large one and one smaller one, clearly designed for a man and a woman. You check next time. I shall be campaigning for equal steak sizes. Gay steaks with the sub slogan, equal meat rights for homos!!' The two had laughed but Max felt sure he had a point.

The journey to Tesco was never a joy for this middle class gay man; the pushing, the lack of manners, the children of already brow beaten parents. Max usually undertook the task at some late hour of the night when only drunks and nurses coming off duty from the local hospital were present. Today though, he would have to go at a peak time. He wandered into the store, took a deep breath dodging a random dawdler who had chosen to stop in the door way to hold a conversation with her equally dawdling husband about whether they should buy pork or beef for Sunday lunch. They were large people and a queue was backing up. A tall and casually dressed man with an inappropriate 'beanie' hat for the summer pointed out to them that they were blocking the 'fucking door.' While Max empathised with his sentiments he felt sure that an 'excuse me' would have sufficed.

He walked down the first aisle, noticing two young women wearing jeans, adorned with sequins and random tearing. They, as Max, were viewing the wine.

'Shall we get a bottle of white wine,' the first young woman asked her friend.
'We have half a bottle in the fridge,' the second young woman replied.
'Well we should get another then. Look at the pictures here, they show you what wine to use with the food you're eating,' the first young woman stated, clearly impressed.
'Yea but what if we're not eating?' enquired the second young woman.

Max walked away shaking with laughter at the young woman's clear yet innocent rebuff of the store's marketing strategy, picking up a bottle of 'on offer' champagne. He meandered towards the flowers. Lilies, white pure lilies, there they were in the finest section. They were ten pounds a bunch. Max thought that three bunches would suffice.

He presented his twenty pound voucher to a woman who had been installed in a temporary unit near the customer services desk. Max stated quite carefully, 'I only need fifteen of this doubled, I'd like to keep the rest of the voucher for other shopping.' The instruction was clear, without being patronising. She took the vouchers and gave Max forty pounds worth of tokens for flowers.

'Excuse me madam, I said I only wanted fifteen of this doubled,' said Max confident that the error could be easily rectified.

'I'm sorry we can't split the voucher,' the woman had replied.

'Oh well Ill have the voucher back and just double the five,' Max offered in what he thought was a generous gesture.

'I'm sorry, but we can't refund the voucher once it's been exchanged,' replied the woman with an authority that belied the fact that she had not had the courtesy of listening to Max's instruction.

'And you couldn't tell me this before I exchanged my voucher, even though I offered you very careful instruction about what I wanted? Max asked.

'You can speak to someone on customer services, it's just over there,' she offered pointing to the counter not eight feet away.

'Strategically placed,' Max observed to the woman who gave no reaction.

Max saw that a lady called Lynda was behind the counter. He had dealt with her before and was still confident of a successful conclusion to this mishap. She had replaced some bottles of scotch and gin for Max almost without argument when the plastic bag in which they had been placed, broke in two in the car park. She looked too elegant for Tesco in some way and Max thought that she would have been better framed in Howells or at a push, Harvey Nicholls.

Max relayed the story to the very sympathetic Lynda who concluded that she would have to get the acting manager as she had no authority to alter the transaction herself. She sympathised with Max at his suggestion that as the vouchers could only be doubled for certain goods, the vouchers ought to come in smaller denominations thus preventing the problem of over committing to a particular range. The manager arrived. He was optimistically called Beau. Clearly gay and one of those gentlemen on whom the term 'manager' resulted in a very over stated self importance which Max was confident translated in any date he was lucky enough to obtain. Eloquently Max relayed the story of the misunderstanding to the manager, Beau.

'I'm sorry sir, once the voucher has been exchanged, we can't refund it, it's company policy,' he stated in a very matter of fact manner.

'I see,' replied Max, 'and did you know that under section thirteen of the Supply of Goods and Services Act 1982, every service has to be carried out with reasonable care and skill?' Max asked.

'I am aware of the act,' replied the little Beau unrepentant.

'So do you think that in not listening to my instruction when offering me the tokens, your member of staff has fulfilled your legal obligations to me?' Max asked.

'I'm afraid it's company policy,' Beau offered yet again.

'Well if it's company policy,' Max raising to a crescendo and people were looking, 'is to ignore customer's requests, abdicate legal responsibility and then just restate that it's company policy time and time again, I think that's horse shit!' Max tone got harsher yet his vowels became increasingly clipped.

'Please don't raise your voice, there's no need to raise your voice,' Beau requested but with no hint of sensitivity in his own voice to the fact that Max had not been heard in the store.

'Oh you're bloody useless you pretentious little queen!' Max barked, 'I'll keep the bloody tokens.' Max turned to notice a group of highly amused old ladies waiting for their lottery tickets. Beau was once again confirming that there was no need to raise voices and Max, carefully dressed from head to toe in Armani, swept out of the store. Dame Maggie would have been humbled by the exit, he later thought.

Cameron returned home three hours later carrying four bunches of Tesco finest lilies. He smirked at Max.

'Was the little man still there?' Max asked.

'I don't know darling,' replied Cameron soothingly.

'OK so I went off on one much to my shame. I could have handled it better but no one was listening and that's so irritating.' Cameron remained silent.

'OK I'm stressed about tomorrow and I took it out on a poor little gay manager in Tesco,' Max looked at Cameron and lowered his eyes.

'I've got scotch for you. Single malt,' Cameron said gently.

'Oh love are you sure you want to make this commitment to me tomorrow. I just want everything to be perfect for you and we're on such a tight budget. There's no fancy hotel as we had first suggested. Its' here and is it all a bit tame?' Max asked.

'Darling, the hotel would have been over ten thousand pounds and tomorrow we will be no more married.' Cameron spoke with a maturity and kindness that made Max contented. He sat at one of the circular tables that had been hired for the reception, the same philosophy towards the guests at their dining table being applied. Everything was ready for the big day. The gazebo now looked festive and tasteful with yellow and white ribbons. The Liberace chandelier accenting the small fairy lights that adorned the door way and reached out to the gazebo. Everything was spotless thanks to Sion and Simon and there, more important than anything else was a wonderful love. Max reflected on his evaluation of marriage. It may or may not be a romantic concept, he thought, but tonight with

Cameron, he felt very romantic and very much loved and in love.

With a child like anticipation of Christmas, the couple locked the back door, placed a snoring Benson gently into his cot, switched off the lights and walked up the stairs.
'Will you marry me?' Max asked.
'Always,' replied Cameron.

Chapter Fourteen

Max and Cameron lay in bed and looked at each other. It was their big day and for once they had woken at the same time.

'How are you feeling darling?' Cameron asked.

'A little nervous,' Max replied.

'Why?' asked Cameron

'I have to open the curtains and see what the weather is like and I just can't bear it.' Max was thinking that all their best laid plans could be swept aside with the onslaught of a typical Welsh summer day. He gingerly got out of bed while an expectant Cameron kneeled at the end of it. Max pulled up the roman blind, heavily embossed in toile de jouy. His heart sank.

'It's raining!' exclaimed Max.

'No!' replied Cameron and ran to the window as if he needed self confirmation.

It was eight o' clock and the happy vision of Benson springing into the room as if he had been self styled maitre'd for the day did not raise Max and Cameron's spirit.

'We could turn the tables into a buffet,' offered Cameron.
'A booffey!' exclaimed Max, with an over exaggerated tone that was one of his favourite lines from 'Frasier' but on this occasion making him sound like Lady Bracknell. 'No,' said Max, it's only light rain. Let's chin it out until midday before we make any alterations to our plans. Come on, I have a small surprise for you.'

The two men and Benson ran down the stairs as if the promise of Christmas presents awaited them. Cameron was not disappointed. On the small table in the gallery, Max had placed a very elegant breakfast setting adorned with champagne, croissants and a small wooden box. Cameron beamed and Benson clearly overstating his position as co-ordinator for the day attempted to sample one of the croissants. He failed.

'Well sit down and I'll get some coffee,' Max said and Cameron still grinning complied. 'When did you do all this?' he asked.

'At around five this morning,' Max confessed. 'You were sleeping so peacefully and I wanted the day to start with something a little special. It was cloudy when I woke but I had such expectations. Now look.'

'What's in the box? asked Cameron.

'Open it,' replied Max.

Slowly, Cameron lifted the lid on the small tortoise shell box. His mouth fell open.

'It's your diamond pinky ring,' he gasped and held it straight up to the light, the eight encrusted diamonds catching even the dull light from outside.

'I couldn't afford an engagement ring and when I got your size from Crouches I made a little trip back with it, got the size altered and got it cleaned. It's not to go on your wedding finger, that's all a bit too traditional, but you can wear it on your little finger. We had to guess the size to some extent but I hope its right.' Max smiled with satisfaction at his partner's joy and knew he had done the right thing. Cameron ran through to the kitchen, gave Max a huge hug and promised to always wear it.

'I am all yours,' he told Max.

'Good,' replied Max, 'I'm selfish about you.'

Cameron placed the ring on his finger and with a slight forcing it fitted well. Cameron jumped a little and gave Max another hug.

As they sat down for breakfast, Max's mobile phone rang. It was Simon, 'Hi, you're up then? He asked with a chuckle in his voice. It was more a rhetorical question as he knew Max often rose before dawn and there was no way he would still be in bed at nine in the morning especially on this day.

'Indeed we are' replied Max. 'When are you coming over?'

'We'll be there by twelve. See ya' later.' Simon sounded excited. He had offered to drive Max and Cameron to the ceremony, driving Max's car.

'I think he's more excited about driving the car,' Max told a still beaming Cameron.

Simon loved cars. He had had over forty of them but was never satisfied. It wasn't that he went that far in one. In fact only four thousand miles last year and he owned a motor bike which Max felt sure was an attempt at regaining youth. Simon had a stash of leathers in his wardrobe, which Max had christened the Suzi Quatro closet. Simon had once taken Max to London and offered to drive Max's car. Max, Sion, Cameron and Simon had all got in and Simon, beaming with the opportunity of driving the six series BMW forgot his basic starting moves and nearly took them straight into an on coming bus. Neither Sion nor Max had let him forget this or the sense of pride Simon showed as he was thumbed up by cute boy racers on the M4. 'It's the car,' Max told Simon after yet another toot from an optimistically entitled Astra, 'I don't think they are interested in us.'

'Are they still wearing the jeans?' asked Cameron.
'As if the weather wasn't worrying me enough,' replied Max. The rain now eased but the sky still cloudy. 'We shall just have to forgive them.'

The morning was punctuated with text messages from the London boys, Marcus wishing them both a happy day and hoping that the weather would be fine. Dr Charles recently upgraded to an i phone sent them a musical attachment playing 'Here Comes the Bride,' which caused both amusement and Max to frown. It was twelve o' clock when Gerard managed a message: Have fun! That was it.

It's both amazing and reassuring Max thought that morning how such an occasion can give rise to a natural increase in atmosphere and joy in a home. As he and Cameron began to get ready for the ceremony, calls from prospective guests confirming that everything was OK, baths being run, caterers arriving, Benson being playful and Max and Cameron exchanging the odd kiss meant that by midday, the house was looking perfect and Max and Cameron were looking appropriately elegant.

'Hi Max, I'm Ivan.' Max turned as he stood looking at the display in the garden. There before him was a very handsome young man with a broad smile, blue eyes and a very neatly cut head of blond hair walking out of the kitchen.

'Hello,' said Max genuinely startled by the young man's beauty. 'Do I keep you under the sink?' Perplexed but remaining very polite Ivan replied, 'I work at the hotel with Cameron and I will be working with James today as your waiter. Did you know I was coming?'

'Yes of course.' replied Max offering a hand, 'Cameron said you would be here at twelve. How are you? I hope everything is here you need.'

'Oh yea,' replied Ivan, 'you have a beautiful home.'

'Thank you,' replied Max. He looked at the young man and smiled to himself. Eighteen months ago, this man would have raised more than just a smile in Max but today he looked at him and was just pleased that Cameron who had been responsible for hiring the waiters, had done exceptionally well. James was dark haired, and beautiful, Ivan blond and beautiful. Max had told Cameron that beautiful waiters were a must and Cameron had surpassed himself.

There was a knock at the door. 'I will answer that for you,' Ivan offered obligingly, his east European accent making Max feel both charmed and guilty. It was Simon and Sion. Max saw them in the distance and noticed Simon's face. It looked like an owl trying to break the enigma code; eyes out on stalks and lips pursed.

'You met Ivan then?' Max giggled as he asked this.

'Can I come in again? replied Simon.

'Oh behave,' answered Max and embraced his friend with a hug and an overly affected air kiss each side of the face.

'He's beautiful,' Simon commented looking around to see if he could catch another glimpse of his greeter.

'Yes and he has a child. I feel old. He can't be more than twenty two.' Max told Simon this just in case his dear friend had any great expectations but also because he felt genuinely concerned that while in his home, no one would be made to feel awkward or embarrassed.

'Darling you are old,' Simon observed.

'But I don't falsify the fact,' Max retorted giving Simon a very knowing look. Simon looked down and suggested a drink. When he and Sion had met Simon was forty. As this was perceived generally as the winter of 'dis' 'consent' when you began to become invisible in the gay community unless you owned a small island, Simon had told Sion he was thirty eight. Sion, the commensurate accountant however had noticed Simon's driving license and did the math. Seven years later it still made no difference, they were as strong as ever.

'A great idea, let's open some bubbles,' Max exhorted as he saw Sion, hugged him, and nodded to Ivan to open a bottle. Cameron then appeared looking very preppy in his blue blazer with white trim, grey slim cut trousers and one of their Parisian shirt purchases. Smiling infectiously, Ivan opened a bottle of Don Perrignon (an indulgence Max had promised his close friends) and they all took a needed drink.

'Well aren't you looking beautiful,' Simon commented, mostly to Cameron, 'two very contrasting styles.'
'Yes Cameron is a preppy sixth former, while I'm country gentleman,' replied Max in his tweed check. 'I could end up on a very different register today if I'm not careful.'

As the four friends and, Max thought surprisingly, Ivan giggled at this, the prospective ceremony was reviewed detailing Sion and Simon's role. As they had just reached the issue of signatories, there was another knock at the door and this time Ivan announced that Marianne had arrived. She walked in holding what looked like a miniature totem pole of sunflowers.

'Hello dear, Charlotte and I wanted to make a contribution to the reception so we saw these and hoped they would bring out the sun.' Marianne walked in wearing a white trouser suit. She looked as elegant as ever. 'Not looking good for her age,' as Max had once corrected a third party observer, 'that mitigates the compliment. She looks good at her age. Language is such an important tool.' The jacket was bejewelled with sequins and mock gem stones and very decorative. Max was so pleased that he had invited Marianne to the civil partnership. In spite of her occasional lack of circumspection and her penchant for travelling in the Far East which prompted Max to declare her eccentric, she always made people smile and took a genuine interest in other people's welfare. Charlotte had inherited this trait and Max felt lucky he had such women on his side.

'Marianne, you look wonderful,' Max declared. She did.
'Thank you my dear it's my memorial tribute suit to what's his name.' Marianne put her hand to her head.
'What's his name?' asked Max touching her arm gently and frowning slightly as if to enhance a power of osmosis.
'The American,' replied Marianne, 'you know the dead American.' Max referenced in his head everyone from George Washington to Michael Jackson stopping briefly with the idea that it could be Liberace but thinking better of saying so.
'Elvis Presley,' Marianne declared.
'Oh that dead American,' Simon interjected, 'yes I see that.' The four friends looked at each other with a slight

disbelief as to the previous two minute's conversation before Max changed the subject.

'Marianne, the flowers are beautiful,' he commented and he was genuinely touched by the gesture. He received the arrangement kissing Marianne on the cheek and placed them at the back of the reception tables by the raised border. Within ten minutes, the rain stopped and as if bewitched by the flowers, the sun not only came out but began beaming on Max's south facing garden.

The pre civil partnership grouping stood in the garden room as the clanking of the caterers was heard from the kitchen. The tables under the gazebo were so elegant with their white cloths, shining glasses and yellow flowers. It was elegant and understated. It was ironic, Max thought, that a budget restraint had produced such an appropriate setting for Cameron and his wedding day. The clock in the sitting room, an heirloom from Max's grandfather struck one.

'Time to roll,' Simon announced.

Chapter Fifteen

Time and therefore timing is of the essence in all of our lives and it is time and therefore timing which can mould both our expectations and determine our outcomes. We cannot change time and therefore when we try to change the timing it is ultimately in vain. Shakespeare explains this when he writes, 'There is a divinity which shapes our ends rough hew them how we shall.'

Mineral silver, the named colour of Max's BMW six series was today looking gold. Max thought that the name suggested an organic overture which belied its polluting six cylinders. When it was cloudy the car looked silver grey but today as the sun reached further west, the stronger suggestion of gold created a carriage like effect as Simon with his head high in the air drove the pillion Max and Cameron to their civil partnership. As they drove along Boulevard de Nantes, the only other contribution with a Parisian element to the day after Cameron's shirt, the car turned into Park Place and then passed the museum where Simon's skills as an architect were now also historical. In front of them stood City Hall and this time Max and Cameron would be entering by the front door.

Max noticed some of the guests arriving. He saw Alan, wearing a kilt and Stephen in a festive light blue suit, no doubt a product of his amazing ability to find a bargain. Michaela looking elegant in her promised black and cream hat and of course Marianne, not tempted it would seem to break into 'I'm All Shook Up' entering the stately building. Max then noticed his mother Einwen. She wore a blue trouser suit. It flowed with a suggestion of eastern style. Max looked at her. She seemed pensive as she walked in with Aunty Jayne and Max hoped that it was joy and not duty which brought her here.

As Max and Cameron decamped, they were met by the elegant Gail Price-Thomas who introduced them to the celebrant Mrs Geraldine Robinson. The woman was charming but had an air of no nonsense about her that could have tamed an under achieving school with one pejorative look. It was ten to two. Max's head swelled with anticipation and nerves as they were led into large reception area.

'OK,' Mrs Robinson began, 'I will go through with you what your roles are today and how the service will be conducted.' She was clearly the sort of woman who had given the country an empire, thought Max and her seriousness was reassuring. The last of the guests hurried past up the stairs as Max and Cameron shared one last moment together as single men.

'You still want to marry me?' Max asked.
'I do,' replied Cameron.
'Hey keep that for upstairs,' Simon said, overhearing the moment.

The clock in the tower of City Hall was a device which usually told the whole city that another fifteen minutes had past in the day. Today though at two o' clock, with the guests seated in the circular Old Council Chamber its chime, with the reverence of Dickens pen denoting the arrival of the first ghost for Mr Scrooge, seemed to create a stillness as Max and Cameron fronted by Sion and Simon walked through the small dark foyer and into the chamber. Max looked at their jeans which had been beautifully accessorized with similar waist coats and plain but colourful ties. 'Lesbian chic,' thought Max to himself. Pachelbel was mitigated by the shortness of the walk and the speed with which Max and Cameron walked down the aisle. Nerves and slow walking are not interchangeable concepts. They stood in front of the now beaming Mrs Robinson. She began.

'For Max and Stewart, this partnership today . . .'
'Its Cameron Stewart,' interrupted Cameron which brought universal giggles and made everyone relaxed. Whoops, thought Max. Mrs Robinson, apologetic but stoic continued.
'For Max and *Cameron* this partnership ceremony today is a proud confirmation of the love, respect and true friendship that they share. Many of you have a special relationship with one or both of them and your presence at this ceremony gives significance and support to their partnership. They now wish to offer each other the security that comes from legally binding vows, sincerely made and faithfully kept and they would like to thank you all for being with them on their special day.'

Mrs Robinson then turned to Max.

'Max, will you take Cameron to be your lifelong partner?'

'I will,' Max replied prematurely.

'Let me finish the rest first,' Mrs Robinson said with a giggle that was now replicated by all of the guests. Max blushed and smiled. Two errors, there surely had to be a third.

'Max,' continued Mrs Robinson again, 'will you take Cameron to be your lifelong partner, will you love and respect him and be honest with him? Will you stand by him through good fortune and adversity and be faithful to him as long as you both shall live?'

'I will,' answered Max. He thought about the enormity of the question and his reply and it was so easy for him to say it. Cameron went through the same question replying, to Max's relief, in the affirmative.

'Max I understand you have some words that you wish to share?' asked Mrs Robinson.

From inside his jacket, Max pulled out an exert from Professor Maya Angelou's 'On the Pulse of Morning' introducing the poem with detailed reference to the woman's title which he thought was disrespectfully ignored by many in the interests of informality.

Max had watched the inauguration of President Clinton and had marvelled at the beauty of the Professor Angelou's mastery with words. Her inclusive attitude declared a moral intention in the world that placed the woman in a league of her own. Black, disenfranchised, and a woman, this lady chose faith, chose love, chose forgiveness and as Max had flippantly evaluated to Simon who asked why he had chosen her work, 'Well she one of mommy Oprah's favourites.'

Max began:

'Cameron thank you for being my civil partner today. I want to share with you and our family and friends some words which I think represent how I feel about our future together. Thank you my darling.' Max then recited the abridged poem.

'From Professor Maya Angelou's On the Pulse of Morning

Lift up your eyes upon
The day breaking for you.
Give birth again
To the dream.
Women, children, men,

Take it into the palms of your hands.
Mould it into the shape of your most
Private need. Sculpt it into
The image of your most public self.
Lift up your hearts
Each new hour holds new chances
For new beginnings.
Do not be wedded forever
To fear, yoked eternally
To brutishness.
The horizon leans forward,
Offering you space to place new steps of change.
Here, on the pulse of this fine day
You may have the courage
To look up and out upon me,

Here Max had altered the poem slightly to dedicate himself to Cameron in a way he knew would make both of them stronger. He composed himself. 'I will be your Rock, your River.' Max stopped. He knew if he said another word at that moment he would cry. He gave himself time to breathe. He heard the still of his family and friends in the background willing him on. He relaxed his shoulders and tried again.

'Your rock, your river, your Tree, your country. (Success!)
No less to Midas than the mendicant.
No less to you now than the mastodon then.
Here on the pulse of this new day
You may have the grace to look up and out
And into your sister's eyes, into
Your brother's face, your country
And say simply
Very simply
With hope
Good morning.

Max's voice croaked as the words, 'Good morning,' were said. He smiled at Cameron and tears ran down his face. When the congregation realised that the extract was at an end, their family and friends stood and applauded. Max held Cameron's hand tight, his face motionless except for tears that for some reason had their own reaction and flowed generously down Max's cheeks.

Mrs Robinson, looking moved by the poem and the moment, gave the men a moment to regroup. She then asked, 'If there is anyone here who knows a just reason why Max and Cameron cannot be joined in this civil partnership you are to declare it now.' Max turned towards the guests frowning as if to say, 'Don't you dare.' Simon coughed and winked at Max.

The legal vows that followed were spoken with misty eyes as Max and Cameron exchanged the rings from the indefatigable Crouches declaring that they knew no legal reason why they could not form a civil partnership. The ceremony was complete and as Max and Cameron gave each other a modest kiss on the cheek, the music of Maria Callas singing 'La Mamma Morta,' from Giordano's opera 'Andrea Chenier' signalled that it was time to sign the paper work. Max looked at his mother and thought about the music. Had he killed her? She looked at him, her eyes reddened and she smiled.

As Max and Cameron signed the register nearly everyone in the room produced a digital camera. Max had never been an enthusiast about pictures. Recording the past was at odds with his optimistic views about life and he also felt that his childhood had been picture after picture such was the vanity of the world of ballroom dancing. Today though, he basked in the attention with relief beginning to show on his face. He and Cameron were a poised middle class couple with their future ahead of them and they looked at their family and friends with the same pride that Max had felt the first night they had declared their intentions at the dinner table in Max's well researched abode in Llandaff.

The post ceremonial festivities included greeting everyone that filed out of the chamber and the obligatory pictures. One with Sion and Simon, one with Cameron's family, looking a little disappointed after a taxi driver, fresh from the middle east had taken them to county hall from their hotel, a building four miles away with a brutalism in its architecture that prevented any aspiration to it being a vessel for a ceremonial occasion. Max's family, abbreviated in number but important nevertheless was next followed by the group photograph under the approving, Max felt, auspices of St. David himself.

Max was overjoyed. Leanda had arrived from Manchester and Max saw immediately that she was six months pregnant. Max hugged her. 'We have the full set now,' he declared, 'gays, straights, family, friends, foreigners and a child en ventre sa mere.'

'What the hell is that Max?' Leanda enquired, her condition highlighting her radiant face.

'It means you're pregnant in French and in certain aspects of UK inheritance law,' replied Max with affectation in his voice. Leanda rolled her eyes. She and Max had shared his home when she lived in Cardiff for two years and had without doubt been a model tenant and Max hoped, life long friend. How wonderful of her to come.

Max reflected on some of the pictures before he and Cameron left the building. He was pleased so many children had come. They might be the generation which saw prejudice as odd, very odd indeed. Max saw how mannered people were making an effort. He paused. He knew that he was marrying later in life. Robert hadn't wanted to; he was of a different generation and in any event the opportunity for Max had only been around for five years. Robert had been dead for four. He felt suddenly very grown up and how gracious that on this special day he received the validation from the people who had grown to love him in a way he had never received from his own family. Max and Cameron were now civil partnered and Max declared to himself that it was now his *time* to be a married man and that he would be a worthy man in this civil partnership.